CW00520799

COMPELLING: *"Laced with vivid snatches of flashback and memory, this emotionally charged novel is raw and vulnerable, but also told with the confidence of a skilled storyteller. From self-healing and grieving to sexual awakening and emotional growth, this novel fearlessly tackles delicate subjects with tenderness and valuable insight."* **- Self-Publishing Review**

BEAUTIFULLY AND SENSITIVELY WRITTEN: *"I very much enjoyed reading it. Author A.D. Pritchard really gets inside the minds and emotional states of his characters and conveys this to his readers perceptively and brilliantly. With believable characters, this is a well-structured story with lots of depth and pace, and I found it a page-turner from start to finish. An author and book you'll be glad you discovered."* **- Hilary Hawkes, Readers' Favorite**

WOW. THIS IS A STUNNER OF A BOOK: *"The Pebble Champion is a grand and glorious debut offering that had me smiling as I read and rueing the inevitable end of the story. I loved getting to know Marmaduke, Chris's iconic and perceptive dad, and vicariously enjoyed every moment Chris spends out at the shore, including those suspense-filled moments as he competes in the Pebble Championships… The Pebble Champion is lyrical and beautifully written; Pritchard built a world that I just didn't want to leave -- not for one moment. His characters fairly leap from the page and involve you in their lives, and it's a grand thing to experience. Easily the best novel I've read in some time, The Pebble Champion is most highly recommended."* **- Jack Magnus, Readers' Favorite**

A RADIANTLY IMPRESSIVE NOVEL: *"Gentle, sensitive, intelligent and extraordinarily well written, The Pebble Champion at last offers a role model for young gay youths to emulate. This author is one of the finest sculptors of the human spirit writing today. Very highly recommended."* **- Grady Harp, Amazon**

THE
PEBBLE
CHAMPION

Alan David Pritchard

First published in July 2013 by
Wilkinson House Ltd

Second Edition
ISBN 978-1-899713-48-6
July 2015

AUTHOR EDITION, 2021
ISBN: 9781691589234

Cover Photo by Will Swann on Unsplash
www.unsplash.com

For Fareed

Surrey Weekly News
Tuesday 24 July 1989

MOTHER KILLED ON M25
Cause of crash 'unknown'

Police are investigating the cause of a crash that claimed the life of a 36-year-old mother from Richmond on the M25 motorway yesterday afternoon.

Sarah Allstrong-Elliot lost her life when her car veered off the road and crashed into the bridge pillar near the Junction 12 Slip Road for the M3. She was pronounced dead on the scene by medics who arrived shortly after.

She was travelling with her 15-year-old son, Christopher, who received serious concussion injuries and has been admitted to a nearby hospital.

Police have ruled out drunk driving as a possible cause and are still examining the area for clues as to the cause of the accident.

"It appears the vehicle just veered out of control," reported one of the investigating officers.

Part One
Letting Go

Thoughts vibrating

"And with the time at 2:45, good morning to those who have just joined us. I'm Mike, the Nightbird, here on London's Heart 201, keeping it mellow, keeping it smooth and taking you through the early hours with the gentlest sounds around..."

The little red lights of the alarm clock pulsate and for a while I almost hear the ambulance sirens again. At three o'clock, I turn on the bedside lamp and squint at my reflection in the window. It's raining hard outside.

I used to know the person staring back.

Then I do hear ambulance sirens, and I remember that this is my last night in the city. My last night here.

"Time," says DJ Mike, "to take a few calls. Remember we're talking about what gets you through the day, and on line one we have..."

My life is compressed into two bags, and they rest against each other as if for comfort. No, they don't. I must get a grip. They lean against each other because I left them there that way.

Auntie Wendy is snoring in the room next door. She's here because she's worried about me being here alone after Mum's death, and she wants to see me off tomorrow morning. *This* morning.

"I try," says a radio phone-in caller, "to live each day as if it's my last."

DJ Mike likes the sound of that, and we blend into a commercial break.

I turn the radio off, and there's a lull in Auntie Wendy's snoring. Although I can still hear noises outside, the stillness inside suddenly seems louder.

It feels like I have a balloon inside me… a balloon expanding, full of tears, and it won't pop: it'll explode, and I'll fall apart and won't be able to control the sadness. I know I should release it; I know that it will be good for me, but I'm afraid of releasing *her* if I let go, and I can't do that yet.

There's the picture of us, taken a year ago when I was 14. There's me, skinny as ever (*Ol' Tin Ribs*, she used to call me) with short, scruffy brown hair and brown eyes, and there she is… with her newly dyed hair and her smiling face. Mum kept that picture on her dresser, and I've put it on my desk. She looks so happy.

If I said she was the most beautiful woman in the world, you'd think I was just saying that because she's my mum and she's dead, and you'd be right, probably. She wasn't beautiful in the way that models are beautiful; she was beautiful like sunsets are. Beauty that makes you think of God and kindness and tomorrow.

That she's gone is a fact, I know that. Every single part of me knows that. So why is it I can't help but wish things were not so final?

Every single part of me wants my mother back.

"I'm leaving and I'm not coming back."

I'm nine, and Mum is at the doorway. She seems to be taking this very seriously indeed, which is good, because I'm determined not to give in. We've had these little showdowns before: I object to having to do some little chore – even at nine years old I know that if I put up a good fight, my mother will realise that it's a lot less drama just to do it herself – and after not getting my way, I usually threaten to leave.

It used to work, but this time she agrees.

"There's the door. Nobody's stopping you."

She even opens the door for me. There is a moment of silence as we outstare each other. Her eyebrows are raised. My arms are folded. Even though I really do sort of intend leaving, I'm thrown off guard by her willingness to let me go so easily.

"I must pack some things first," I say finally, and without looking at her, turn to walk to my room. Once there, I collect the essentials: a small plastic dolphin, a cushion to comfort me, a packet of sweets that I intend eating very slowly, and – out of spite – a photograph of Auntie Wendy. Mum watches me,

expressionless.

"And just where do you think you're going to go?" she says as I brush past her on my way out.

"I'm going to explore the world," is what I would usually say, defiantly, and she would usually reply,

"Well, pack a clean pair of undies then. The world's a big place. And don't forget toilet paper. Nobody'll want to take in a boy whose trousers are soiled."

Then she would usually hug me despite my protests and tell me she would never let me go.

I've threatened to run away three times before. The first time I got as far as the front door; the second, as far as the elevator; and the third, I managed to get to the lobby of our building before turning back because I needed to pee.

"I'm going to find someone who loves me," I say this time. It has the desired effect. She flinches.

"You have no idea how much I love you," she says.

"Well, I don't love you."

If she's hurt by this remark, she doesn't show it.

"Fine," she says. "Off you go. I'm the worst mother in the world and I don't deserve you."

"Yes!"

"So go. I'm still young. I can still have other children who will love me more than you do."

"Fine," I say, digging in my heels.

"Fine," she says, adding, "other children who won't complain when asked to do something simple like empty the dustbin."

"I'm leaving now."

"Other children who won't moan every time they're asked to do something. Off you go then."

I want to say something more, but she suddenly closes the door, and I am left staring at number 87, unsure of what to do next. The corridor windows make the wind groan. The door is shut.

The elevator arrives too quickly. I know she can hear the doors open. I try not to look at the kitchen window to see if she is watching.

"I'm really going," I call out, loud enough for her to hear but not so loud that everyone on our floor knows my business.

The elevator doors slide together and I press G, trying to glimpse my reflection in the stainless steel panels. The trip down seems to take much longer than usual.

My friend John is in the lobby with his mum, and when the doors open, they greet me warmly.

"Look what I got," he says before I can tell them I won't be coming back. He holds up a box filled with cast-iron dinky cars. "What do you think?"

"There's a car-boot sale near the stadium," his mum says. "You should get your mum to take you."

"Wanna play?"

There is nothing I enjoy more than playing cars with John, and the offer is too tempting to refuse. He has been my friend for over a year. He is not as skinny as I am and already has muscles. His eyes are green, and he has blond hair. His mum calls him Surfer Boy. She sees my carrier bag and asks, "Where're you off to?"

I almost tell her, because I know she'll understand, but for some reason I decide not to.

"I was going to play in the park. Can John come with me?"

"Why don't you come to our place instead and I'll fix you both some lunch?" she asks.

We live on the same floor, and when the elevator door opens, my mum is standing there with a look of genuine relief on her face.

"Hello, Sarah. I've invited Chris over for lunch," John's mum says. And that's how I ended up staying. I was going to continue my expedition into independence after playing at John's place, but I felt tired and ashamed. I needed to know that Mum wasn't still angry with me. I needed one of her hugs, and I got one.

After that, we did the chores together.

Smiling, now, feels like a chore. Auntie Wendy has the sort of face that looks happy even when she's sad. She beams at me with a smile big enough to wrap your arms around.

"Here we go."

An abundance called breakfast is lowered onto my lap.

"Can't beat brekkies in bed." She kisses me on the forehead, on the scar left by the accident, and pulls up a chair. "Tuck in."

Her invitation is generous and combined with the aroma of porridge, eggs, bacon, toast and freshly squeezed orange juice, is impossible to decline.

"This is a feast," I say.

"Well, there's more, so get cracking."

"Nobody makes porridge the way you do," I say.

"Hmm," she replies, biting into her toast, "that isn't necessarily a compliment."

"I'm going to miss your porridge."

"Hmm," she says, "that neither." She knows I haven't understood. "As in you want to give it a miss?"

She searches my face for signs of comprehension, and gives up.

"You're grieving. I understand. How's your head?"

When I looked at my reflection earlier I saw that, although the pain had receded, I had a scar and a giant bruise. I lift my hand to feel the swelling.

"It's fine. I mean I'd rather stay with you," I say suddenly, and can feel the burning sensation behind my eyes.

The smile fades, and she puts her spoon down.

"I'm going to miss you…"

"As in…?"

The smile reappears.

"I really am going to miss you, my little big man."

She's always called me her little big man, even though I am short for my age.

"I'm not a big man," I say.

"Oh yes you are. I was in here before you woke up."

My jaw drops. For a while I search her face for signs that she's joking, but her smile seems forced, as if glued on.

"Gotcha," she says, and laughs. "Anyway…" she sips her tea, "you know that won't be possible." Her voice is sad. "You know I'd love to have you."

I can feel the balloon inside begin to inflate again. I have to breathe in deeply. Mum said in her will that, in the event of her passing away, I was, if at all possible, to stay with my father, whom I haven't seen since I was five, and who, for all intents and purposes, is a complete stranger.

That Mum didn't ask for me to stay with Auntie Wendy is a mystery, and I'm not sure how my Auntie is coping with that. She seems to be fine, but I'm sure she finds it as puzzling as I do. She wanted to accompany me down to the Isle of Wight, but I told her that I'd be okay (Mum would want me to be strong), that I was a young man now.

"Anyway, the sea air will do you good. You'll like it down there. Nothing here but smog and traffic now."

"You're here."

"Yes, but you're young. You'll enjoy living by the coast. It's right near the shore, your father's place – two minutes' walk from the beach. Think of all the young ladies in bikinis. A feast!"

She says *feast* with genuine enthusiasm, as if she really thinks I will enjoy living with the man who ran out on my mum and me.

I don't like thinking like this. A part of me is angry with her for not contesting Mum's decision; but I know she means well, and I know I'm not thinking right these days. Instead, I say,

"How are you going to cope without me? You won't last five minutes."

Auntie Wendy has always included me in her life – ever since I can remember. She's treated me as if I was her confidant, her best mate – the one who understood all her secrets. She's even called at two in the morning to spill all the juicy beans absorbed in an evening's socialising. She's invited me to clubs, but I'm too young, and more or less look it.

"We'll write each other regularly, believe me, and you'll only be a call away, so don't think you're escaping from me that easily."

My aunt, while being wholly conventional in the sense that she does not draw attention to herself while in public, has a fluffy way of looking at life, which is appealing and uncompromisingly cheerful. Nothing gets her down, because for her there is a calm and rational explanation to everything; even the unexplained, or phenomenal. Everything happens for a perfectly good reason, and if we can't comprehend right away, life will whisper its truths later when we have learned how to grapple with its lies, or something like that.

Odd how you can be listening to someone while not really hearing them at all.

Auntie Wendy likes philosophy, but she doesn't burn incense or smoke weed or anything like that. She doesn't wear bangles and hippie clothes. She looks like a secretary, actually. Why am I describing my aunt to imaginary people when I should be listening to her right now? I'm not going to see her for a while. This is like quality time, or something.

"… running stark naked down the lobby…"

My expression has obviously changed. Hold on.

She grins.

"Where have you been little fella?"

"It was *big* little fella earlier. And what are you doing running around naked in the lobby? When was this? You didn't tell me about this."

"You haven't heard a word I've said, have you?"

"I heard the naked bit."

"Just checking. Oh, I've just realised. I won't be around to interrogate any of your future girlfriends…"

Remind me to tell you about that.

"Or take you jogging early mornings or… or make you do chores on a Saturday afternoon."

"I know what you're doing," I tell her firmly, "and it's not working."

"Well, you'll find plenty of reasons not to miss me once you get there."

And Mum? How will I stop missing her? Why would I want to?

My aunt has beautiful eyes. Her hair is short, spiky, dyed caramel, and totally unlike mine, which is mousy brown and which Mum let me grow long-ish. I tell you this only because my thoughts have been weird lately. I looked at Mum's photograph for hours this morning and now I can't remember her face.

I tell this to Auntie Wendy as we wait at Victoria Coach Station, and she hugs me, real tight, real genuine, real *her,* and she tells me that this is normal. "Time," she says, and gives the whole spiel about it being a healer. I know that she is right, but for some reason I don't want to hear it. It's not enough; it doesn't ease the pain; it won't bring Mum back to life.

Time seems to bend and snap back, to pass by without lingering, then to shoot forward, so that the present becomes the past, despite holding on to it as hard as I can.

Now the bus is turning at the traffic lights and Auntie Wendy is half a mile away. Now she's gone. Now I'm treating our parting as a memory, as though it happened a long time ago. Now I think I see John, standing on the corner where we used to buy comics. Or rather, I don't see John; I think I'm John seeing me at the window of the bus; I try to imagine what I look like to him and whether he sees through my smile. I don't know why I think this way: John and I rarely speak these days. And the only person on the corner is a homeless person scratching in a bin. Now even this is a memory, a snapshot of goodbye.

Auntie Wendy's jumper smells of porridge and sunshine. John liked to wear a yellow cap, like the colour of the car in the photograph of Mum and me on holiday when I was 14, a year ago – the one I forgot to pack and which, no doubt, Auntie Wendy will keep, or post on to me.

Images of London city life blur past.

Shop windows and favourite stores bring back memories. So many things we did together.

There's the hat shop in Wandsworth.

I can remember her being embarrassed when, in the hat shop one Friday, she picked up a ludicrous example covered in plastic fruit and, placing it in her head, began to laugh at how it looked on her.

"Isn't it simply awful? It's so tacky!"

An elderly, dear sweet old soul tapped Mum on her shoulder to ask for her hat back. Apparently, she had put it down to try on something new.

I remember how we laughed.

Why can't I remember your face?

That has been happening a lot, lately. As soon as I grasp at any memory of her, her face disappears. Sometimes I feel that all this is not really happening to me. I get a sense of seeing myself from a distance, as if this were a movie, and the camera catches the bus and pans with its movement, capturing both the sudden splurge of green as a backdrop, and my face at the window looking out.

Funny, that.

Funny? I'll show you funny.

We were at my grandmother's funeral (his side of the family), and Mum was recounting an anecdote about her. I remember her saying the words; I don't remember the anecdote. Something to do with a wig and a fancy dress party, but that's about all. Or maybe Grandmother arrived at a party thinking it was a fancy dress ball. Funny how, even though we were not close, I can remember her face clearly. I also remember that *he* wasn't there. Even though he and Mum had separated, Mum and Auntie Wendy stayed quite close to my grandmother because, as Auntie Wendy put it, "she's a nutter, that one."

"Shit, dammit – trust the old bat to croak now."

Mum was at Auntie Wendy's, trying to find something black. This was silly really, because even I knew Auntie didn't have any black clothes. It created negative energy, she said, although I think it was more because she thought she didn't look sexy in black. Odd, you'd think sisters as close as that would know the quirky details of each other's lives. They don't, did not, look alike. Mum was fair, Auntie Wendy is dark. Mum had blonde, almost white hair, and you know what Auntie Wendy's looks like. Yet, there are, were, traces of each other in each other. They had the same soft, inviting look; their frowns were similar. I almost have an image of her, like something clear and blurred at the same time; fragments of torn photographs… frustrating because I can almost see her, can almost remember features. Mum found a violent red outfit, and they convulsed in giggles, like the girls in my class. Auntie Wendy went for a fluorescent lime-green ensemble with a matching hat adorned with gaudy imitation fruit.

"Oh, Tallulah!" Mum was bent double with laughter. The hat reminded her of the incident in the shop, and she recounted the story to Auntie Wendy. I remember we all laughed like we had never done before. I can clearly see the fabrics of that afternoon; I think I can almost smell the fragrances. But Mum is a blur.

For the first time in little under a week, I feel strangely happy. It's a mild, muted sort of happy, like when you laugh through tears; except, I'm not crying. I haven't cried. Not yet. Not now. I almost did, at Mum's funeral, but something held me back. Maybe it was the pain? It hurt to cry. I will not let the balloon explode. Am I happy because I can remember? But remembering inflates the balloon, doesn't it? I'm smiling because details are coming back. Because I haven't lost it.

In the church – now don't get me wrong, we bore no animosity towards Grandmother – the outfits were worn not because we wished to mock or insult her memory, it was just that, the way Auntie Wendy looked at it, Grandmother always regarded them as bright, silly characters anyway.

"Funerals are for remembering the laughter and celebrating life. Shithellfirebrimstonecrap, she's gone to begin the next phase of her life, why not send her off with a celebration?"

Everyone else wore black. There were sniggers.

"God bless them," Mum said.

I never got on with my grandmother much. She was too loud all the time and insisted on kissing me at every opportunity. But even I knew she would want a livelier send off. The service was austere. The hymns were dismal.

I remember now. Auntie Wendy sat in front of us and for no reason at all, and never having had any association whatsoever with happy-clappy, evangelical-type churches, proceeded to proclaim a healthy, "Amen, Brother! Praise Jesus!" after every mild statement made by the withering old minister.

"Ethel Elliot was a respected member of our church community…"

I can smell mothballs and old people.

"Praise Jesus, Alleluia, Lord have mercy!"

All coughing and fidgeting stopped.

"We remember her as a kind person, rich in generosity…"

"He's my salvation! Praise Jesus!"

Her hands were in the air while the fruit on her hat bobbed like it was on the back of a South American lorry on bumpy terrain. It was perhaps this image that started me off. I can't remember exactly, but I began to get the giggles, and ever since my voice broke, these giggling fits have become harder to suppress or keep under control. I covered my face with both hands, pressing my nostrils closed with my thumbs. I hoped it would look as if I was crying, especially when my body began shuddering with suppressed laughter. Mum also found giggling difficult to control, and after shooting severe looks at me, her lips began to purse, and I saw, from between my fingers, that she had covered her mouth with her hand, while her eyes –

I can see you, sort of.

– her eyes betrayed her. One peek at the bobbing apples and her body began to shake.

"Praise Jesus! Amen. Let's hold hands."

The rest of the congregation, who admittedly consisted mainly of Ethel's friends from the home, almost simultaneously let out an audible gasp, and looked confused. Theirs was not the sort of church in which handholding was encouraged.

"Ethel can see us now," Auntie Wendy continued. "She wants us to hold hands. Let's sing."

The minister wore a forced smile. There was another moment of sheer silence. Until I snorted, and unable to hold it in any longer, both Mum and I erupted.

Maybe Mum died because we were laughing during grandmother's funeral?

The bus pulls up at a petrol station. Looking at my watch, I see that it is twelve thirty. I've been on the bus for an hour. Did I fall asleep? *Which is the dream?*

Until now the seat next to me has been empty. I say this because a boy, probably my age – I can't tell – gets on the bus. He has scruffy brown hair and bright blue eyes, a slim build and a confident smile. He reminds me a bit of John. Except John has freckles, and blond hair. And John rarely smiles at me these days.

The boy checks his ticket, and then glances at the seat next to mine. He is wearing shorts and a T-shirt. His legs are tanned and only slightly hairy. I turn to look at the people entering the garage shop while he stores his bag and sits down. A pregnant woman struggles to get on the bus. Auntie Wendy and John are two hours away; everything else, a million miles. This is real, being here. We wait for the pregnant lady and a few latecomers, and then the bus moves off.

I wonder if he can tell just by looking at me what has happened in my life. Why do I wonder what he thinks of me? That's been happening a lot lately too. Whenever I meet people, it's never on my terms: I always worry about whether or not they accept me.

He looks at my bruised forehead and says, "Ouch. What happened?"

What happened?

When I wake up, I see Auntie Wendy standing by my bed. She does not have to tell me I'm in a hospital. Her eyes are incredibly sad; I see through the smile. John is at the doorway with his mother. Both are crying. I expect John to say, "This is another fine mess you got us into, Stanley," but he does not.

The boy next to me opens a tube of Smarties. He offers. I shake my head.

"Go on," he says. "They make you clever."

"No thanks," I say, hoping I don't sound too rude.

"So what happened to your head?"

I am about to tell him but then say, "Fell at the swimming pool."

"Looks damn nasty. Here, have a sweet."

I shake my head again.

"So where're you going?" he asks.

"Isle of Wight."

"Is the correct answer! You have won today's star prize." He grabs my hand and pours sweets into it. "Well done, old bean!"

I think I frown.

"No," he says, "you don't understand. Well done!" Then he fishes a cracked and faded sweet from my palm and holds it up. "Old bean," he says, showing it to me.

I think I smile.

"Ah," he says. "You can. I was wondering how long it would take before I got you to smile. It's this thing I do. My name's Darryl. You have a nice smile. Oh, it's gone now. Damn, I'm going to have to try harder. To make you smile, that is. Don't look at me like that. I'm not mad. Who are you? What are you doing here? Speak."

He's the kind of person Auntie Wendy would adore. The kind of person who I would… never mind.

"My name's Chris," I say. "Thanks for the sweets."

His smile has a cheeky, mischievous quality to it.

"You earned them. Well, actually – you haven't. Well, maybe you have, seeing as you're wounded and all. Besides, I'm just being nice. Character flaw of mine. So why are you off to the island? Do you live there? I have a mate who lives in Shanklin."

Should I tell him? He'd probably think I was looking for

sympathy.

"I do now," I mutter, and look out of the window. Wide green fields and small hills burdened by clouds. We have just passed Basingstoke.

Mum met a guy who had a farm, and we went there one Sunday afternoon. I think his name was Anton. He had two sons, and he teased them by showing them a twenty-pound note, offering to give them half, and then tearing the note in two.

"You?"

"No, I'm going to visit my girlfriend," he says. "I'm getting off at the next stop. I wish I lived on the island, though. The sea's beautiful. Do you know I can't swim? Can you?"

I nod.

The water is icy cold; the indoor heating has packed up. Outside it is hailing. Mum has taken up knitting, and she smiles at me from the side. I'm convinced I'm turning blue. The other boys are bigger than I am. I wonder why they don't feel the cold. My teeth are chattering. All I want is to go home. I don't want to learn how to swim, and I don't care how important it is, and I want to cry because the water stabs my skin and I'd rather have a bath. Mum sends encouraging glances and totally ignores my plaintive expressions. Surely she can see the agony I'm in? She has wrapped a towel around a hot-water bottle, and it lures me until it is the only thing I can think of, and I surrender to tears, which makes the other boys laugh.

"One day," Darryl says," I'll have my own swimming pool. I've always wondered what it would be like to swim naked underwater in the moonlight. Have you?" His remark catches me by surprise.

"Have I wondered about it, or have I actually done it?" I ask, unsure where this is going.

"Both."

"Swimming naked is nice," I say.

"Really?" He looks genuinely interested, impressed even. I know I'm lying. I can swim, but I have always worn swimming trunks. Up until now, the thought of swimming naked has never crossed my mind. "I've often dreamed of being stranded on an island with a lagoon full of dolphins," he continues, moving on to another subject, tilting more sweets into his mouth, and says, while chewing, "That would be so cool. I wonder if they have dolphins at the aquarium on the island? You should try to find out. Be cool if they do. I love dolphins. They're my favourite animals. Fish. Are fishes animals? One day I would like to swim with them. Dolphins. They're the most incredible creatures. I wish I were a dolphin. Dolphins don't have to do homework and chores."

"Or have to clean up their rooms."

"Precisely."

"At least dolphins can swim," I say.

"Hey? Watch it." He grins and leans back. "Or a bird. I'd like to be a bird. Imagine flying. Soaring. I'd shit on Jason Grant's head. He's this cretin at school. Do you smoke?"

For some reason, I like the way he looks at me. "No."

"Good. He does. I hope he dies. God, I hate him."

"Sometimes I hate you."
"You'll get over it," Mum says.

"Do you have people like that at your school?" he asks.

"I'm starting at a new school soon. We had our fair share of shitheads back at the last one." I add, "But they never bothered me." *Liar, liar, liar.*

There are three boys chasing me, calling me names. After a while I try to drown out their words – such cruel words – and I pretend I am a spy escaping from the Nazis, like in that film Mum and I saw on telly… but I cannot pretend that John is not one of them.

I'm aware that I'm being defensive and I've no reason to be so. He is very open about his life, or so it seems, and friendly enough, sincerely so. I'm pleased he is doing most of the talking, but I'd rather remain mysterious; the way most other boys appear to me when I first meet them, mysterious in the sense that their lives seem to embody secret forays into adulthood; lives that I haven't yet lived

– the world that Auntie Wendy talked about. I know what it is. I want him to think that I'm enigmatic. Can a short guy with big ears and a small nose be enigmatic? I told you my thoughts are weird these days. Here I go again. Wondering what people think of me.

"How old are you?" I ask, although I don't know why.

"15. You?"

I tell him my age, he nods, and we start a conversation about nothing in particular. He's very pleasant company: easy to talk to, funny, a good listener. Conversation is fluent; there are no awkward gaps of silence. I think it's because he's interested in everything he talks about. While he talks, I get the impression he can cope with anything. Like Auntie Wendy, he seems to possess the ability to take things in his stride. He's very likeable, enviously so. When he stands to collect his bag and say goodbye, I find myself – his grin and handshake are genuine – hoping he'd stay.

Nobody else gets on at his stop, and we wave goodbye as the bus pulls off. There are sweets on the floor.

Now this is a memory, and while I'm pleased for the company, the emptiness that remains when he gets off is amplified by my circumstances. His seat is empty. I'm alone again. I think I miss his company because it took my mind off things, but now I have to deal with his absence as well as everything else. To my shame, I conclude that it would have been better not to have met him at all.

It has become quite overcast. Dirty-ashtray clouds threaten more rain. I try leaning my head against the window, but it's like having a pneumatic drill as a pillow. I imagine my thoughts vibrating, getting confused and muddled. I wish I were a cow. There are a few in the fields. All they do is stand and chew. They are not bound by the emotions that life inflicts upon us. They are just cows. They'll be slaughtered for their meat. Actually, I don't want to be a cow. I want to be a dolphin – I think of Darryl – curious that he should talk about swimming naked, but I know what he means. It's the feeling you get underwater, where your mind allows you to be anything free. That's what I want to be – anything other than me. Don't get me wrong. I'm not filled with self-loathing. Put yourself in my shoes. I'm going to meet a man who is supposed to be my father. I do this only because it is what Mum wants... wanted... wants. This will be the second time I've met him in ten years. The first was at the funeral. I'll tell you about that later. Right now, I don't really want to think about him – or what to expect when I get there. I don't really want to think about anything actually, because thinking inevitably leads back to the awful truth.

I cannot accept that Mum is dead. A part of me believes this is all a dream.

Before, if I had a headache, Mum would bring me an aspirin. If I had toothache, she'd take me to the dentist. Immediate relief was always at hand. But there are no tablets for this. No instant remedy. Nothing can ease this pain. I'll use it to keep me from collapsing.

"Irreconcilable differences," was the term I remember Mum using when I asked her why my father left. "It means we no longer got on. You know how sometimes you and John fight, and then you make up and are friends again? Well, your father and I weren't able to be friends anymore."

"But why? I don't understand."

"You will one day."

But I wanted to know then. One day is too far to wait for answers to childhood questions – like why adults cry. I hardly ever saw Mum weep, and when I did, she'd say in her kindest voice, "I'm learning to let go." When she first said this, I looked for something in her hands, trying to find what she was letting go of – but there was nothing. "You'll understand one day," she'd say, pulling me closer to engulf me in one of her special hugs.

Surely, if you're hanging on, letting go means falling?

Time to sleep.

There is a scream from the back of the bus. No. Shouting. People are shouting. Someone's in pain. I can hear her cries. I sit up sharply and turn to look. A man rushes down the aisle calling for the driver to stop.

"Driver, are we close to a hospital? There's a woman in labour back there. We need a doctor!" He turns to the rest of the bus. "We need a doctor!"

The pregnant woman is groaning.

"This hurts!" she exclaims between gasps and deep breaths.

Four or five passengers crowd around her, but I can't see her face because the backrests are too high. The bus slows down and another woman – she has a large black afro – shouts, "Don't stop, you fool. Get us to a hospital!"

"If this is a prank…" the driver warns.

The pregnant lady's distress cries are sufficient to convince him. I can see her now. They have moved her to the aisle. She's about 20, I suppose. I don't know.

"But I don't want to be late," someone says.

"Stand back, give her some air." The Afro lady has taken charge. "Driver – step on it!" To the others: "Stay in your seats." To the pregnant woman: "Just breathe deeply, my love, keep breathing deeply."

"The nearest hospital's about 40 minutes away," I hear the driver announce. Then everyone begins shouting directions, and people are telling people to get back, and a little girl starts crying.

After 38 minutes, we have still not arrived.

"Christ, I don't think this baby can wait. Jesus, we're going to need some water and towels, or a blanket… anything. Don't worry my dear – I've given birth six times…"

"I have towels!" I call, reaching for my bags. I have two towels. They have my name on them. For some reason I find that useful, as if I expect to get them back. Soon they are passed along, along with bottles of water (sparkling and still) and an old jacket.

"We're almost there now," the driver shouts.

"But I am going to be late," someone says.

"Oh, shut it," somebody else replies.

"Deep breaths, you can do it."

"It hurts! Jesus-God-Almighty it hurts!"

"Deep breaths, come on."

Everyone is demonstrating the technique to her; they look as if they all are giving birth. There is a lot of heavy breathing going on. I catch a glimpse of the woman - her eyes are screwed shut. She grits her teeth and groans. Then she screams at the top of her voice – a piercing, chilling wail. It sounds as if she is gradually being torn apart and there is nothing any of us can do. Well, the Afro lady seems to know what she's doing.

It's a remarkable sound, the cry of a new-born baby, and when it comes there is a loud cheer. Even I'm cheering. The woman has tears of joy now, and she cradles the bundle with extraordinary tenderness. Her pain is a memory. It's a boy I hear.

He can keep the towels.

The day I met John, he was wearing a towel pretending to be a caped superhero. I met him at a scrapyard behind a service station near the park next to our block of flats. School had finished early that day, a Thursday – something about a bomb scare I think, and Mum could not get away from work. Auntie Wendy came to fetch me, and on the way home I asked if I could play in the park. It was a devious scheme. We had just recently moved. Mum was panicky about letting me play anywhere unobserved. I knew Auntie Wendy wanted to watch something on television, so I stood a reasonable chance of being let out alone.

I soon tired of the swings and seesaw in the park and decided to have one last slide before going home. I saw the hole in the fence as I slid down. It led to a small gully filled with beer cans and rubbish, and then up a slope to the scrapyard. There the wrecks of cars were piled upon each other – Minis, Volkswagens, Renaults, Fiats, and BMWs – a menagerie of mangled metal.

I had seen our car from the bathroom window that morning. It had been dumped on top of three Toyotas. I cannot begin to describe how I felt. But I did not cry.

The reporters are here.

I have a hard time holding them back. They surge forward, almost toppling me over.

"Mr. Elliot! Mr. Elliot! Is there any truth in the rumour that you intend going through the fence sometime today?"

"Has this ever been done before?" A woman-reporter with red hair forces the microphone to my lips.

"Do you realise the risk you're taking?"

"No-one has ever gone through and come back to tell the tale," somebody says.

I smile contempt at them. Don't they realise?

My agents force the media back to behind the swings. I breathe deeply. This is not going to be easy. Sure, others have tried – and failed – but I'm not like the others. Stay in the zone, I tell myself. Stay in the zone.

"Oh, my God!" someone shouts. "He's going to do it!"

I can feel the blood surging through my veins; adrenaline builds up. I have to leopard-crawl through the hole and then stay low to avoid being seen. Easier said than done, though. The hole is just a few feet ahead; I can feel the dust at the back of my throat. Coughing would give me away completely.

"You can do it! Go on!"

"Yes, I can see him now, Paul – he's almost at the fence… no, no – he's made it to the fence… he's stopped… I'm not sure what's happening… it looks like he's moving backwards… no, no – he's going forward now… I don't believe it… he's going through… almost… yes, he's made it!"

The trench is littered with old bomb shells and bits of debris. I remember the words of my commanding officer – "For God's sake, don't step on the shells with the red stripe!" – just in time to lift my foot away from the striped landmine. Suddenly, I understand what the expression 'walking through a minefield' means.

This looks impossible. I knew I would have to jump across, rolling to the right of the water pipe (rigged with explosives; they couldn't fool me), but the jump would leave me exposed for at least two seconds, which was too long to be exposed to enemy fire.

"Of course he knew this would be a problem long before he set out. If only he had someone to cover him."

"You know Chris Elliot always works alone."

I remember the jump in slow motion, the thud as I roll past the pipe, missing it by millimetres; the heavy pounding of my heart when I realise I've made it. There are three tanks just behind the hill: secure cover if I'm fast enough. No time to think.

Move move move.

"He's made it to the shelter of the tank on the far right. Of course, he'll have to destroy anyone inside before moving to the control tower. He can't risk enemy fire on the way back."

"Wait a minute – there's someone else there too!"

"Where?"

"Behind the lorry on the other side of the camp. It looks as if he's armed. Can't be much of a superhero if he's armed. What'll Chris do now?"

I'll tell you what Chris will do – he'll stay low, that's what. As far as I know, I haven't been seen. My mind races for a strategy. Surrender is never an option. I check to see if my handgun is loaded, and then do that sliding motion I've seen in movies.

I edge forward to have another look. He's still there, but looking the other way. This is going to be easy. Quickly, I fit the telescopic lens onto the barrel of my gun and drop to my haunches. Soon I have him in sight. He's about my age, I reckon. Tragic waste of young life. I watch him for a while. Poor fool. Amateur. My finger rests on the trigger. Wait – is that a white handkerchief he's waving? Have I been seen? No, he's just blowing his nose. Now's the perfect time. He looks at me just as I pull the trigger. I will always remember the look of alarm on his face. I know it will haunt me the rest of my days.

He clutches his heart, struggles with his footing and falls over backwards. The One-Shot-Wonder does it again. Actually, falling over backwards is a neat trick, unless he just slipped because I gave him a fright – in which case it means he's probably hurt himself and it's my fault. Is he going to stand up? No. For the first time in my nine years on this planet, I say the grown-up word *shit*.

I run to where he has fallen only to find no one there. I saw him fall with my own eyes. This is supposed to be *Rambo*, not *The Twilight Zone*. Maybe I only injured him, and he's rolled somewhere to die?

"Drop your weapon!"

For the second time in my life, I say the grown-up word *shit*. My enemy's eyes widen. "That's a swear word," he says, screwing up his face.

"I'm a US Marine. I'm allowed to talk like that."

"Well I'm Special Agent John Hunter, and you're under arrest."

"And I," said a voice behind us, "am Commissioner Wendy Allstrong. You're both coming with me."

And that's how I met John, aged nine.

It is raining. The bus has finally reached Portsmouth Harbour. Time to meet my father, aged I don't really know.

No reason not to

The ferry to the Isle of Wight is late. I overhear some of the other passengers moan that it is becoming too regular an occurrence. In a way, I don't mind. I am actually nervous about meeting my own father.

When the boat finally arrives, and we make our slow way across the Solent, I cannot help but think of the movie *Escape from Alcatraz*, which Mum and I saw on telly one Christmas Eve. The water is a murky clay colour. The town of Ryde is in the distance, and, as we near, I glimpse a crowd of people waiting on the dock. I realise that even if he were there, I probably would not be able to recognise him.

I know what you're thinking, but no, I'm not going to behave like a real shithead and treat him as if he is my enemy. He may have left Mum and me, but she forgave him, and I know this is her last wish, so out of respect, I suppose, I'll give it my best shot.

Maybe not. I'm a teenager. I'm allowed to be fickle.

I do recognise him. He's standing at the top of the pontoon, holding an umbrella and a sign. It says:

KRIS.

I kid you not.

He has mousy, wild, shoulder-length hair and a look of deep relief. He looks so young; and he can't spell my name. He's grinning. His eyes don't smile.

"Hey, Kris," he says, as I approach. His voice is deep and gentle. "I am sorry you had to wait a while for the ferry. It has a reputation for being… tardy."

I explain about the delay on the coach.

"We had to make a detour on the way. Some woman gave birth on the bus."

"What? Really? On the coach? Good grief. Well, I'm pleased you're here safely." He stares at my forehead.

"It doesn't hurt anymore," I say.

We begin to walk towards the station towards a brightly decorated train. He explains that it used to belong to the London Underground and that the island uses it because the overhead bridges are too low for normal-sized trains.

I look across at the old Victorian-style buildings of Ryde beachfront and wonder which is my new home. When I ask him, he points to the last station mentioned on the line on the sign inside the carriage. A town called Shanklin. My new home sounds like a meat dish. He says it will take us 20 minutes to get there.

"You spelled my name wrong," I say along the way. This comes out more harshly than I want. He shrugs.

"No, I didn't."

No grin. He looks serious enough to make me not want to pursue the matter. He stares me straight in the eyes.

"This is how it appears on your birth certificate. Sarah didn't like it, so she changed it on all your other forms. I wanted something less biblical."

When we arrive at Shanklin station, he reaches for one of my bags. I let him take it. There's no need to be a martyr. I don't know what I'm supposed to say.

"The apartment's not far." His tone is gentle. He smiles. "It's just around the corner in fact."

It turns out to be a bit further than that. We walk for ten minutes down to the beachfront. The rain is coming down hard, and by sheltering me, he is getting half of his body wet.

His apartment is one of four surrounding a courtyard and a swimming pool encased by doorways and little patios. The apartment is on the upper floor behind a blue balcony. Before we enter, I stop to stare at the bay before me. To my left is a long stretch of sandy beach revealing a pier in the distance and chalky white cliffs way beyond that. Straight wooden structures stretch from the sand into the sea. To my right, more wooden structures and what appears to be the remains of a pier. It juts out and then abruptly ends, with a large gaping gap with the pier head isolated some distance away. It's as if something has taken a bite out of it. It's as if something should be there, but isn't. Along the esplanade are a few hotels and some beach huts. Then the bay curves with dramatic cliffs topped with trees. The grey sky ahead seems to merge with the sea. Time has stretched again.

I can't speak because the balloon inside suddenly inflates, making my eyes smart, making me bite my lip most of the time. As he opens the door, I hear him say, "I know it's not going to be easy, for both of us. Despite what you may think, I cared very much for your mother…"

I have to hold on… something inside… I mustn't cry…

"I think you'll like the place. It's quite… I don't know… cosy, I suppose. It's comfortable, and when the weather's good…"

A part of me wants to bolt, to go home, to go back to Mum and Auntie Wendy and John and my life. I must get a grip.

"I've taken this week off to spend with you, but we have to go for an interview at your new school next Tuesday."

I follow him inside, half hearing his words.

Like I said, it's nice, it looks nice… I don't know. It's spacious, not badly decorated – filled with modern abstract paintings.

Don't let go.

He shows me to my room, which is furnished with a bed, a desk, and an alcove looking out at the sea.

"It used to be my guest room but I have never had guests staying over, so – I thought, instead of – you know – my doing it up – I… I thought, maybe… I could help you decorate it to suit your taste." He turns on a small table lamp. "You basically have carte blanche – it's a blank canvas really… er… make yourself comfortable – I can get you tea if you want… a beer?"

A beer?

"I'm… I'm not thirsty… thank you."

"Well, okay – " a brave smile, "I'm… well, I'm going to make a brew for myself. I'll let you unpack."

And then from nowhere, I ask, "Do I have to? Right now?"

"No, of course not."

He places his hand on my shoulder and then pulls it away quickly.

"Let me show you the rest of the place. This…" we walk through to a large room with big bay windows, "… is my studio." He opens the blinds and the place explodes in colour, and easels, and giant canvasses, and sketches and bits of sculpture and paints everywhere.

"I… I didn't know," is all I can say. The place is incredible. Imagine a mad artist's studio and you'll get the picture. The space is small but well-lit and incredibly busy.

"Well – here's the thing… um… any of my work… outside of this room… is open to your appreciation or criticism – but… I really must ask you this… I need this space… I have not lived with anyone for… for a long time."

As I listen, I can't help but want to put him at his ease, but I don't know how. He continues almost nervously. "And… well, I'd appreciate it if you only came in here by appointment."

"Sorry?"

"This room is out of bounds. I'm not going to lock the door or anything… it's just… when I'm in here, I mustn't be disturbed…"

You're already… no, don't.

"… at all." He manages a smile. "I won't go into your room without your consent, and… vice versa?"

"Okay."

I'm not sure what else to say. I am not sure what to do. And even less sure where to go.

"Good. And now – the sitting room."

So I follow him. He leaves the studio door open. The sitting room is painted a peachy apricot Moroccan style, and there are bright cushions everywhere. TV and a VCR. So far, so good.

"This room is never out of bounds. If your grades are decent, I'm not going to hassle about how late you go to bed. I… I don't go to sleep early, myself, but… yeah – do your best at school… and all that… fatherly shit. This is the sitting room. The kitchen is through here…"

It's cosy, the kitchen – lots of wood.

"The mural on the wall is a view of what you'd see if there wasn't a wall. I finished it last week. The mirror behind you," – I turn – "is not a mirror but a painting of a reflected sunset; so's that one – but it's sunrise." He points to what looks like a mirror above the microwave. It's an amazing kitchen.

I actually like the place. If the kids at school could see it...

But home was home and had Mum.

"I sound like an estate agent," he apologises. "Apart from my room, this is it. What do you think? I'm sorry. You look tired."

Tired?... tired... this is a really cool place, but it's too... too far away, suddenly, from home – where memories are etched into the walls. Where even though Mum was gone, there was something of her all around in every room. I need that now. I need something to keep me from feeling like... My father seems all right. This is a fantastic place – it has everything, a video, a decent sound system, amazing art, a computer, a view...

Get a grip, Christopher.

"You sure you don't want something to drink? I think I, we, have hot chocolate."

I notice the wrinkles near his eyes. He's not as young as I thought. At the funeral he didn't look young at all. He looked a wreck to be honest.

I remember now. He had a wild beard, and dark glasses – then, when he came to see Auntie Wendy and me to sort out Mum's will a few days later, he shaved the beard and looked in his 20s. I think he must be near – 38? 39? Not 40. No. He hadn't shaved his beard then. This is the third time, not the second, that we have met. Why is my memory so muddled? Why can I remember meeting John when I was nine, but not my own father a little over a week ago?

"Kris?"

He has an unusual way of dressing, but I like it. Casual-indifferent, Auntie Wendy would call it.

"I'm sorry – what were you saying?"

The concern on his face reminds me of Auntie Wendy.

"Look," he says, gesturing to the couch. "Put your feet up." He sits cross-legged and runs his hands through his hair. "I don't know if anything will... make sense now... or even later. I know that words are not going to help, and I'd hug you if I thought I was allowed... so... I know you must be hurting big time, and believe me – if there is anything… anything that I can do to make things… to… sit down, please. Make yourself at… make yourself comfortable."

When I do, he smiles.

"If I could bring your mother back…"

My eyes are burning.

"It's okay," I say, as if warding off his words with my hands. "This is just hard for me, that's all."

I'm surprised at my honesty. I don't want him to think I'm looking for sympathy.

"I understand," he says.

No you don't. How can you? You're not me.

Stop these thoughts, Christopher.

I spy something with my little eye. A collection of vinyl albums.

"I thought I was the only one who ever listened to Peter Skellern," I say, moving to the corner where the records and CDs are stacked. Here is a revelation. Nobody at school knew about this – I kept Peter Skellern a secret for obvious reasons. They were all into chart stuff. "I don't believe it."

"You're a fan?" His eyes light up.

"I have most of his stuff on cassette in my bag: *Astaire, Still Magic, A String of Pearls.* I enjoy the way he takes music from long ago and recreates the sound today. It's not old-fashioned or stuffy. It's like a lot of it is tongue in cheek. You know?"

Mum has bought a new evening dress for a work function. She instructs me to wait while she takes off her tracksuit trousers – she tells me to stop staring at her cellulite.

"I'm a teenager, Mother – I'm supposed to stare at a woman's undies. It's a boy thing," I tell her.

She replies, "Look on, then – but remember this. Enjoy your youth. And no matter which girl of your dreams breaks your heart, take comfort in knowing that cellulite will avenge your pain."

"I like your legs – they're not bad for someone of your…"

"Careful, Sunnyboy."

"Mother, you have lovely legs."

"Hmm. I bet you say that to all the mothers you meet. Go put on some Peter,

36

and I'll get changed in the bathroom."

I choose 'The Continental', and Mum soon appears looking radiant and glorious and splendid. She dances like a flapper (that is what women dancers were called in the 1920s) and gets me to join her.

"You are so dashing," she says as we twirl around the lounge. "You're going to break many a girl's heart one day, I think."

Funny how I remember those words, but while I can see her dancing – absolutely crystal clear – her face is never in focus.

He has other stuff I like, too. Like Tom Waits and John Martyn. Mum liked John Martyn. She loved his deep voice. Auntie Wendy introduced me to Tom Waits, whose voice, she said, sounds like a tractor chewing gravel. She used to read the lyrics out loud from the sleeve insert before playing her favourite tracks. "Pure poetry," she'd say, after.

"No Donald Fagen," I say, and realise I'm smiling.

"Only *Nightfly* – but that's in the studio. You're a Donald Fagen fan? Aren't you supposed to be into Rick Astley and Kylie Minogue?"

"Oh, please."

He grins warmly.

"I think we're going to get along just fine."

If that's what you want to think.

Stop it, Christopher. For Mum's sake. Mum. Dad… no – he's still a stranger.

"I'm going to unpack." I stand up.

There's a look of confusion on his face, which softens, and he nods.

"I was thinking, maybe we could go out to eat tonight? I don't really feel like cooking. Give you a chance to know the area."

"Sure," I say. "But later. I'm not very hungry."

There's a moment's silence, as if one of us should say something. Then I make my way to my room and shut the door.

I've been staring at my two suitcases for nearly half an hour. I can feel the balloon.

I suddenly feel terribly, terribly alone.

Unpacking the clothes is easy. I have three or four shirts and trousers and a couple of jumpers. I've never been into fashion, even though you have to be to fit in at school. Without the right labels, or designer gear, you're virtually a nobody. That was the source for a few rows at home: me pestering Mum relentlessly for the latest fashion accessory. Then, on my birthday two years ago, after I had saved up for a really expensive jacket I had wanted for a while, and which I really wanted to wear to the school's Casual Day, Auntie Wendy, Mum and I went shopping.

Oh, I had saved up quite a bit for that jacket. It was the pinnacle of near-teen clothing perfection as far as I was concerned. And I knew that I would be the envy of virtually everyone in my year group. But even determined saving wasn't enough – both Mum and Auntie Wendy had to make a sizeable contribution. I can still feel the excitement, holding all that money in my hand and knowing that a dream was soon to come true. Perhaps what Mum had said was right: the expectation is often more thrilling than the getting. And then, when they had watched me go straight for what I wanted, Auntie Wendy remarked that she couldn't believe the prices of clothing these days. Oh, you should have seen my face as I approached the counter with my valuable purchase. I was so happy. Just as I was about to hand over the huge wad of cash, Mum stepped forward and interrupted the transaction. She politely told the cashier that we would return shortly, apologised, turned to her sister and said, "Sorry, Wendy, I can't let this happen." Now, I have thrown mighty terrible tantrums before, but I knew, as Mum herded my open-mouthed 12-year-old body into the sunlight outside, that the mother of all tantrums was about to erupt. I was stunned. I was confused. I was bewildered. I was fuming. Auntie Wendy tried coming to my rescue.

"Sarah, you did say he could buy it."

"Mum, why are you doing this?" I said, aware that soon I would not be able to control my outburst.

"It costs as much as a week's wages, Wendy. It's obscene. And for what? So he can fit in? Rubbish."

"But Ma!"

"But Ma nothing. Don't Ma me now. Come. Both of you."

She marched us, oblivious to the barrage of complaint, to a store nearby, one that was over-zealously proclaiming to be – of all nightmares – a factory outlet. The indignation was too much. I stood firm.

"I'm not buying anything from this place, I'm telling you now."

Echoes of all the school jokes made at this shop's expense – it was a standard insult that so-and-so buys his/her clothes from the factory outlet – rooted me to the spot. Even just to be seen loitering near the premises was enough to damn me.

"I'm not going in, I'm telling you."

So what does Mum do? She instructs Auntie Wendy to ensure I am not mugged, disappears into the store, talks to a shop assistant and then emerges holding, in plain view, a pair of Disney-inspired underpants.

"If Mohammed won't go to the mountain," Mum mutters, and holds the offending pair of pants up before my face. "Whaddayathink? Gorgeous or what? Now, Chris – do you prefer… this… or would you like…" And from almost nowhere she produces another pair of pants, equally cringeworthy. "Or would you prefer this pair? No? Okay, I'll get some more." Then she disappears into the shop again. My eyes were darting to and fro in a desperate attempt to make sure this little spectacle had not been witnessed by anybody from school. When she appeared again, holding up girls' frilly pink garments, I decided for the sake of any reputation I might have had at that point to join her.

When we finally left the store, I had, in assorted bags, bought: two pairs of jeans, three T-shirts, five pairs of socks and a pair of half-decent trainers. Oh, and a chain for my neck. And I had cash left over to buy a CD, and some ice-cream at that new place in the square.

Every now and then, I notice, I stop and find myself staring at nothing. The photograph album is under my tapes (all six of them), and the few books I want to keep. There's the book of poetry by a man called Stephen Dobyns. Aunty Wendy said I'd like it because he's obscure. She's right. I like his poetry because it doesn't sound like the poetry we are forced to learn at school. But I don't understand all of it. The other book was given to me by my mother for my last birthday. It's by a woman called Julia Cunningham, called *Burnish Me Bright*, and is about a mute boy who is treated as an outcast in his village. He is befriended by an old man who teaches him how to communicate through mime. Although it is very sad, Mum and I read… have read it together at least five times. We were forever reading to each other. I haven't opened that suitcase yet.

I try not to think of anything, while being aware, for the first time, of a… a closing in all around me. Not a force, but it is as if the air is being squashed, like mist entering through a window, filling the room until it seems as if it can't hold any more. The suitcase suddenly feels enormously heavy, and each item of clothing (neatly folded by Auntie Wendy) seems almost impossible to lift, as if each is a rock that I have to carry to the cupboard.

The last item from suitcase number one is the first jumper Mum ever knitted for me. It's big, fluffy, blue and green and is supposed to be the solar system with some of the planets. Except that her skills were not that refined then; she chose an ambitious project, the final result being an overly large concoction of wool, oozing colours – like one of my father's paintings, the pattern discernible only if one employs incredibly giant leaps of the imagination. The more I look at it, the blurrier it becomes. I've unfolded it and laid it on the bed. Her hands knitted this. Something drops to the floor.

It's happening. It's okay. It's me.

I remember when I first tried it on.

Her hands knitted this.

I can feel her tugging it over my shoulders and see her grimacing at the length of the sleeves.

When I put it on now, I see the something on the carpet. It's the photograph I thought I didn't pack. The one from my room this morning. Mum is smiling up at me.

I pick it up slowly and hold it in my lap.

I can feel the balloon.

I can't stop the balloon.

The pattern on the jumper is beginning to wobble. I look at her face and see all the details I thought I had forgotten. Her hands knitted this. I can only see her if I look at the photograph. I look up to catch my breath.

It's okay, darling. I'm here.

Details fade from my mind's eye. It was taken after a football game last year. We won. She had been the loudest supporter in the crowd of reluctant parents forced to give up Saturday mornings in bed to chauffeur their kids to matches.

No, not now.

This is all a dream. This is all a dream. Please, Jesus, let this all be a dream. The design on my jumper seems to float on water. The pattern is absolutely clear: there's Saturn and her rings; there's fiery Mars; a moon with exaggerated craters. What was she thinking as she knitted this?

Mummy.

Not now. She hasn't gone.

I'll never see her again. I'll NEVER ever see or feel her again.

No. Please, Mummy. Please don't be dead.

Oh, shit. I'm crying.

I'm so angry you have left me, and I love you with all of my heart. I want you to be here so I can tell you that; that I love you so much. I want you to put your arms around me and tell me a story. I want you to cradle me like a baby. I want to scream and shout and punch God in the face.

Oh, God. This hurts. I feel so alone. The balloon has exploded with more impact than I had anticipated. (When my father knocks on the door some time later, I don't hear him at all.)

If this were the ocean, I'd expect to find more fish, and it takes a while before I grow accustomed to being underwater. I'm not floating; I'm not swimming. Like some planet suspended in space, I neither sink nor rise. It is very blue down here, very quiet - hauntingly serene; poignantly isolated. I'm alone, and I'm not scared. I don't have to breathe. I don't have to move. I don't have to cry. I sense that Mum is somewhere. I know she is not close, but she's there. Then from out of the blue void, a shadowshape appears.

The dolphin swims and looks at me with its head slightly to the side. It looks happy to see me, and, almost in slow motion and without any thought whatsoever, I reach to touch its snout.

Pure smoothness.

The dolphin turns and swims below me before shooting past and far above where I watch it leave the water only to return a few seconds later. It swims around me a few more times, slowly, and then comes to my side. I take hold of the fin. We move through the water together without rushing. It is only then that I realise I'm completely naked.

I wish Mum were here. John would like it too. And that other boy — whatshisname — Darryl. I want them all here because I want to share the happiness I feel.

Mum is fuming.

"What do you mean you lost it? You can't have lost it. No, no, no, Christopher — you have not lost it. Where did you last have it? Jesus, Christopher, that was this week's rent money!"

I'm crying and trying to say I'm sorry, because I know I really have lost her purse. She looks so angry. I keep expecting her to smile and tell me that it's bound to be somewhere in the house, but she knows I went out to play with John in the scrapyard, and I know it was in my jacket. We have already scoured the scrapyard for the jacket. She stomped and became semi-hysterical. She has never shouted at me like that before. And all the while I kept saying, I'm so sorry, I'm so so sorry. She will have to work more overtime and miss out on her birthday party.

Another time — that look of disappointment when she came home to find I had not cleaned up, and her boss was coming to dinner.

I don't deserve this happiness.

The dolphin drops beneath me, and I'm left on my own.

"Well it's true, I could have been much nicer to her. I let her down so often."

The dolphin returns without a smile. It is grimacing. I can't breathe. The water is suddenly freezing cold, and there's something eerie about the way that dolphin is looking at me.

Dolphin?

Shark.

Someone has put his or her arms around me. When I open my eyes, I find that my father is here.

"It's okay. It's just a dream."

If this is a dream, then why am I still crying? Why can't I stop? Why can't I stop?

I don't have enough reason to push him away, and he holds me while I cry myself back to sleep.

I wake up once in the night. He is asleep in the chair by the window, his sketchbook on his lap.

He's the reason I'm crying now.

Enough.

He is not there when I wake up in the morning. It's a completely different day. The sun has not yet risen. From my window I see that there isn't a cloud in the sky, and the strip of beach that greets me is bathed in soft early morning light. I feel drained and numb, but I don't want to go back to sleep. I slip on a pair of tracksuit bottoms and trainers. I find a pen and paper near the phone and scribble this note:

Don't be alarmed. Gone for a walk.

I've not yet been given a key, so I decide not to lock the door on my way out. There's an odd moment, as I step out of the courtyard and cross the road to the beach, when I think: maybe things are not that bad.

But, like I said – just a moment.

The burden of sadness has not left me. However, I'm pleased I'm not still weepy, and I must admit it was a bit embarrassing last night. I've never cried like that before, and while Auntie Wendy (I must phone her today), had she seen me, would have nodded "go on – let it out", I don't think I'll be doing that again in a hurry. I had no idea crying could be so painful.

It's six-thirty am. Wednesday. No school 'til Tuesday. The air smells of salt and new beginnings. The waves sneeze, sending a faint drizzle into the air. A clump of seaweed litters the shore. It's not warm enough yet to take off my shoes, so I make my way along the shore, taking care not to get too close to the water. Fresh air. The sound of the sea drowns the morning traffic.

I walk past a stone cottage nestled in the crook of a cliff. *Fisherman's Cottage* is a restaurant bar with a thatched roof and a few small fishing boats parked before it. Further along, there is an area with pebbles that opens up to an expanse of sandy beach recently washed by the morning tide. I make my way down towards the rocks.

A gull lands nearby and pecks at something in the crack of a rock, before peering at me inquisitively.

"Do you talk?"

"Yeah, I'm not like the others."

"Where are the others?"

"Flown off to catch fish. What about your friends?"

"Probably still sleeping. What's flying like?"

"Cold."

The gull flies off to become a speck and a smile on my face.

John had a parrot that repeated words spoken by Auntie Wendy. Its favourite saying was "piss off", but it couldn't quite manage the shithellfirebrimstonecrap she recited frequently. John has to go to school today.

Actually, a part of me is glad I'll be starting at a new school soon. Apart from John, I never really got to make many friends. Everyone else seemed to live enormously exciting lives while I was content to stay in the company of my mother and my aunt. Not that they sheltered me. It's just I liked my own company. Besides, John is, was, my main companion. We spent a lot of time in each other's company up until a year ago.

Before it happened.

I used to like playing at his flat when we were younger because he had so many comics and toys, and we often lost ourselves in fantasy games where we would re-enact action sequences from movies or books. I say up until a year ago, because puberty has chucked in big time (that is only one of the reasons) and he's found himself a girlfriend. Now his fantasies are of an entirely different nature, and he is beginning to sound like all the other boys at school.

I had a girlfriend too, but Auntie Wendy scared her off – remind me to tell you about that later – and to be honest, while I know that relationships are an adventure soon to be embarked upon, right now I'm not really that interested in having a girlfriend. I'm interested, in a way, but just not now.

I liked playing football with mates from school or going to movies with Mum or the theatre with Auntie Wendy; playing monopoly on a Sunday afternoon, listening to music in my room and then rushing to read the song lyrics to my mother while she cooked dinner.

When something is there and real and tangible and then suddenly vanishes, you feel like you're being pushed over a cliff into complete darkness. I look across at the damaged pier, but instead of seeing the remaining parts, I contemplate the gap that remains. What was real is now dream-like, and the unknown presents itself as invisible yet unmistakably life-like.

As I look into the rock pool, I wonder if the creatures within it communicate with one another as the day begins. Does the starfish wake up and stretch and yawn and groan at the sprightliness of a shoal of small fishes? "Morning, morning!" they cry as they swim past in formation. The crab shoos them off as it sweeps its doorway, and moans about all the sand. Don't go near the crevice, warns the snail, there's something lurking below. "Bloody foreigners," they all moan when the tide rushes in.

You are the best mother in the world.

I suddenly feel extremely hungry.

Which is good, because when I get back to the apartment, Marmaduke is making breakfast, and the smell of freshly buttered toast infuses the air.

"Enjoy your walk?"

It's seven-fifty. I nod my reply.

"It's beautiful out here."

"It has its charms. I never liked living in the city."

"How long have you been here?"

"About three years."

"How come you didn't contact us?" I try not to make this sound like an accusation, but I don't think I succeed. I'm surprised that the question slips out and immediately apologise. He looks alarmed.

"It's okay. You must have many unanswered questions. We'll get round to them all. Let's just take it one step at a time. Anyway, how do you like your eggs? I don't know if you eat bacon."

"I'm starving."

"Tuck into the toast then. The eggs'll be ready soon. Sunny side up?"

Sunnyboy.

45

And so we begin the day with conversation over breakfast. We don't talk about her. Instead, I ask him about the damaged pier and he tells me about the great storm which ravaged most of it two years previously. He points to a painting he made of it shortly after it happened. I ask him about some of his other paintings. There are canvasses leaning against the walls, hanging on the walls. I wish I could describe them accurately. There are what look like alien vistas, underwater scenes, liquid landscapes, or just, as he explains, emotions expressed through colour and form, although the form is difficult to categorise. They are undeniably captivating.

I stare at his face as he explains when one was painted and why, and wonder how much of me is discernible in his features. This is my father – the man I've tried not to miss for many years, and faintly recall feeling sad and confused at his absence. You see – I remember little of him – I know he was there at the beginning, and as I said, my recollections of his leaving when I was five are muted and indistinct.

There were times at school, when other boys talked about their dads, that I felt as if I was missing something in my life. Perhaps this became a seed of anger occasionally watered, but he was never real enough to hate intensely. I remember moments when I wished I had a dad. I know I resent him for the times I caught Mum crying on her own, but maybe I misread the situations. I find as I listen to him speak now that there are few reasons to dislike him. He seems friendly, and nervous, but kind – his voice is surprisingly deep – he enjoys talking about his art. I'm listening, but his voice washes over me. All I hear are meaningful sounds.

My whole life is changing and there is nothing I can do to prevent it. I will have to get on with my father because there is no reason not to; not now, now that we've met.

I'd be lying if a part of me did not admit to being quite taken in by the plush unusualness of the apartment and its proximity to the sea. I shouldn't really be thinking thoughts like this. I'm not a materialistic person, although I had wished Mum and I had been richer. We didn't have a video machine, or a fancy sound system and modern kitchen. Now that I think about it, it does seem odd that Marmaduke was living a seemingly comfortable life while Mum and

I always seemed to just get by. I don't recall Mum mentioning anything about his paying support.

I don't know why I'm thinking about this now.

Like I said, my thought patterns are weird lately. I think sometimes I must be slightly mad. Thoughts and emotions aren't that easy to control. Even my body is conspiring against me.

"Very good, Graham – very effective."

Graham beams and folds the little slip of paper he had virtually crumpled while trying to say his English oral presentation before a non-too-interested class.

"And now it's…" Miss Emerson runs her finger over the register list, closes her eyes and asks Graham to say stop. Her finger rests on my name. "Christopher," she says.

I've prepared my work. I practised in front of Auntie Wendy last night. But I cannot stand up. And let me tell you this. I'm accustomed to waking in the morning with a hard-on. It does not make me blush: it's life. Auntie Wendy even jokes about it in front of almost-girlfriends.

Anyway, what I'm not accustomed to is its tendency to creep up on me at school, even when my thoughts are not remotely sexual in nature. And I know, if I stand up now, everyone will know I'm standing up now.

"Christopher?"

My mind races through images of nuns and toilets and old ladies' sagging breasts and dog-poo and cellulite.

He's quite animated, my father. He uses his hands a lot when he speaks. For a while I try not to listen to the words, but see if meaning can be gleamed from the gestures. It's a silly exercise and reminds me of the time Alice and I tried using sign language to communicate answers in class tests. We thought we had it down to a fine art: to the world I was scratching my chin with two fingers, to Alice it meant Multiple Choice, Question Two, Answer C. The only problem with our system was: we each relied on the other to actually do some studying, and neither did, so all we actually ended up doing was giving each other the right signals to the wrong answers.

"I was thinking," my father says, "if you want, I can show you around town. Help you get your bearings. Shanklin. The area's bigger than it looks."

I nod.

"That's if you're up to it. If you want to stay in, I… well, whatever. This is your home now. We could go to a movie if you like. I'm sorry, it sounds like I'm trying too hard."

"Do you have a girlfriend?" The question comes out of nowhere.

"Not anymore," he says. "I'm celibate now. Besides, there's not much room for intimate relationships when you paint as much as I do."

"Mum told me you were a painter. I thought she meant that you did walls and skirting boards. Not art."

"Your mum never really got to see the successful," he gestures to the canvasses, "side of my career. I did plenty artwork in the beginning, but my career only took off after… we split up. It was one of the reasons why we split up. It's more complicated than that. I don't know how much she told you… about us, or about why I left you…" He pauses and looks down. "Let me just get through grieving, before going into all the explanations."

He's grieving too.

"I thought I wouldn't…" *I must make sure this comes out right.* "I thought I would hate you, or something. Or that I'm supposed to, or something. But, I don't. Mum didn't tell me everything, and to be honest, I think she was waiting until I was older. I know this is what Mum wants. I'm not going to give you a hard time. Tell me what you need to tell me when you feel the time is right."

This is the most I had said since we met, and I'm pleasantly surprised at how mature it all sounds. Mum would be proud of me. I'm going to make her proud of me.

Marmaduke nods. He says the word *time* again, and sighs. Then he asks, "Do you paint?"

I tell him about my attempts at school. "I didn't like the idea of expressing my feelings and allowing the whole world to criticise or pass comment. It's like writing poems: fine for me to read, but not anyone else. I never knew if I liked what I painted, so I didn't think anyone else would."

"You need confidence, and that can take a long time to find. It took me a long time."

"I think your work's good. I don't understand it, but it captures my attention."

"It's a matter of knowing what to look for," he says, rising to collect the plates.

I get up too.

"I'll do the dishes," I offer.

"Relax. This is going in the dishwasher. Yes, well, we might as well get this over now. As far as chores and stuff like that is concerned, I've one simple rule. I won't leave things for you to clean up if you don't leave stuff for me to clean up. And if we can help each other out every now and then, well, so much the better."

"Cool." It sounds reasonable. "How do I earn pocket money?"

"How much do you normally get?" When I tell him, he says, "I'll treble it."

My jaw drops.

"And what do I have to do?"

"Simple," he says. "Just stay out of trouble. It's going to take a while to adjust to having someone around all the time, and I don't want to spend this time with you stressed out because you did something irresponsible or spectacularly stupid. You don't need to let me know where you're going or necessarily what you're doing. I'm cool about most things. Just let me know when I can expect you home. I hate having to worry. And if you're planning on experimenting with anything, talk to me first. There's nothing you'll be offered that I haven't tried. If you can be responsible, your pocket money's secure. If not, you'll have to find a part-time job." He says this with a smile. "So now we have the ground rules sorted, what would you like to do today?"

"Christopher!" Auntie Wendy is overjoyed to hear my voice. "You nutty little scoundrel. How's my little big man?"

"Today, fine. Yesterday – not so good."

"I know. I called last night, but you were sleeping. The first few days will be the hardest. How was the trip down?"

I tell her about Darryl and the birth and the rain.

"Oh, really?" she says. "Someone gave birth? God, Christopher, you don't waste any time." She giggles.

"My only contribution was towels. I was polite. I looked away. To be honest, it all looked a bit gruesome."

She laughs at this.

"But isn't that marvellous? You're off to start a new life while a new life starts off. I think it's an omen. Oh, that's priceless. Oh, you are lucky."

"Lucky?"

"Everything's an adventure for you, Chris. New beginnings."

"Adventure? You mean nightmare."

"Only if you choose to see it that way."

"What about... Mum?"

"Oh, Chris – she's still with you. You'll always carry a large part of her with you. And she's watching you right now. I know she wants you to be happy. How are you getting on with Marmaduke?"

"He's actually quite nice. He's an amazing artist. You should see his stuff. He took me to so many places today. You know he actually has some of his stuff exhibited at the local art gallery? And we went to this amazing little bookstore. I... you'd like it here."

"Oh, good. Then you won't mind if I visit every now and then?"

"Serious?"

"Of course. I'm your Auntie. I'm contractually bound to check up on you. That's my job. You're not getting rid of me that easily."

This is good news.

"When?"

"Soon, don't you worry. Or as soon as that crabby old boss of mine grants me a holiday."

We laugh at this. I know she runs her own business.

The water is warmer than I expect; the waves, gentler than this morning. The evening light is golden. Marmaduke and I have come for a stroll to watch the sunset. He tells me that for him the beauty of the scene is in how the world responds to the light, not the light itself. He points at the buildings along the beachfront; how their colours change hue to reflect the evening; how the windows suddenly become jewels. Even people change colour.

Someone's dog runs past. Kids are playing with Frisbees. Lovers hold hands. There's a game of volleyball. My father and I talk little. We've spent the day talking, and our silence is comfortable. At Fisherman's Cottage, we meet a friend of his – a woman with a small baby; she seems friendly, and they start up a conversation.

I wander over to the rocks, waving to the toddler every now and then. I roll up my jeans, trying not to slip as I walk through little pools, collecting shells and pebbles. The beach has collected a large crowd, and I'm pleased about the bit of privacy that this area offers. The rocks form a natural tidal pool, which, now that the tide is out, lies still, reflecting the evening sky like glass. I take a pebble from my heavy pocket and wipe the sand from it. I like its smoothness and wonder how it got so shiny. Then, glancing at the water, I hurl it across the surface. It skims and hops three times before disappearing with a plop. Three times.

I can do better than that.

I take out another and try again. One, two, ah. Another try. The trick is in the wrist action, I reckon. Okay, watch this. Like a professional tennis player in slow motion rushing to the net, executing the perfect forehand, I twist and throw my arm forward. The pebble bounces off the water – once, twice, three times…

The world holds its breath.

Four times!

Hey, way to go, Christopher!

Surface like glass

I'm a camera again: a high angle shot of a busy motorway. Two lanes. We are following a Fiat; yellow, with a dent on the rear bumper. A bumper sticker: 0-60 in three days.

Through the back window we see a woman driving and a teenager in the passenger seat. From their movements, it is clear they are singing along to something on the tape deck. The boy turns the music louder; his mother turns it softer.

It's been a reasonably eventful couple of days. Marmaduke has shown me some of the local hangouts, my favourite of which is a place called The Chine. It's a forest-like area cut into the cliff that runs along Shanklin beach: a wooded coastal ravine, with shady walkways, a little waterfall, tropical plants and cages with birds and chipmunks. The path that leads from the top of the cliff takes us down to the Heritage Centre, where Marmaduke shows me paintings by Turner and the scenic works of Victorian artist Lefevre James Cranstone. He talks about these artists with such interest that I cannot help but be interested too. It is nice not to have to speak.

One of the paths leads down to the Fisherman's Cottage, another takes you up to a vantage point where the whole of Sandown Bay opens up to reveal the wide expanse of the sea. From here you can see the white cliffs of Culver Down. I ask Marmaduke if he ever paints up on the white cliffs, but he explains he prefers absorbing a scene outside, and then painting it from memory. He says something about not wanting to be tempted to paint photographs – meaning, photographs would capture the views perfectly, but he wants to express his response rather than painting landscapes.

Over dinner at Fisherman's, I meet a few of his friends.

"I don't have many, I'm afraid," Marmaduke says as we walk in, "just a couple. It keeps distraction down to a minimum."

There are three people at the table when we arrive: Sylvia, a woman of about 40 who apparently lives below us and whose clothing sense can best be described as antiquated; and two men, Andrew and Graham, both bald and each wearing a large silver raindrop-shaped earring. They are all really friendly, but I suppose that's because of my circumstances.

I think Sylvia likes Marmaduke. She keeps looking at him, over dinner, when he isn't looking. She agrees with everything he says, sighing in all the right places. She tells me he is the finest artist she has ever met. She says I have his eyes.

"At least," says Andrew, interrupting, "you don't have his name."

Marmaduke feigns indignation. "There is nothing wrong with my name."

"Sure," Graham adds, "if you're a dog. Or a budgie. Dear," he says, pointing at me, "just be grateful he never named you Rover."

"I like my name," Marmaduke says. "It's different. Did you know it means Lord of the Seas?"

"Lord of the RSPCA," Graham mumbles, but we all hear him, and we all laugh.

I notice that he has his hand on Andrew's knee. I look twice to make sure, then turn my attention to Sylvia, who is staring longingly at Marmaduke. He goes on to explain that, although he was teased as a kid about his name, he grew to like the uniqueness of it and found that it helped establish his name as an artist. To be honest, I'm not really listening.

When I tell my father about Sylvia's apparent infatuation later, he just smiles. He says that she belongs to a different era; and, while her body is in the present, her attitude resides firmly sometime far ago. As if I know what he means. I ask him if he fancies her and he laughs out loud.

"No, no, no," he says. "I adore her to pieces – she's a real individual – but there's no spark… no sexual chemistry between us." Then he asks me what I thought about Andrew and Graham – it became obvious, as the evening went on, that they were a couple – and, as a reply, I shrug.

"They seem nice," I say. "When they told me they were partners, I thought they meant business partners."

Marmaduke laughs. "They're that, too. They've been together longer than you have been alive. They were the first to be brave enough to exhibit my work here on the island. You're not freaked out, are you?"

My response is no lie.

"Please," I say, "Why should I be? And besides, I have more important things to worry about."

The deputy head teacher of my new school smiles at me patronisingly. "It's never easy starting at a new school," she says, "but we pride ourselves here on the warmth and companionship that forms part of our school spirit."

I imagine if Marmaduke were to paint this scene there'd be lots of vomit.

"We're a family here, and you'll fit in really well, don't you worry. With your academic record, I don't foresee any problems."

Marmaduke is doing his best to look the part. He's dressed smartly, and he's shaved. I think he's a bit uncomfortable.

The school building is impressive and not very far from where we live; it looks well-equipped, and the grounds are big, well maintained. It looks a bit like my last school, which looks a bit like every other school I've seen. The pupils are having lessons now, so I haven't seen anyone other than this instantly dislikeable woman, Mrs Flank – I kid you not.

"And if," she adds, leaning forward. I think she'd take my hand if she could. "If you need to talk to someone, my office door is always open."

I glance over my shoulder; her office door is closed.

I nod, and nod again, because I really don't know what to say.

"Anyway," she says, "I've assigned someone to be your mentor, as it were, for the first few days, so you shouldn't feel too alone tomorrow. He's a lovely boy, very bright, very friendly. He'll show you the ropes."

Funny, I'm entertaining images of ropes now.

She concludes her talk by asking me if I have any questions.

Actually, yes – why are you so nauseatingly friendly?

Why did my mother have to die?

Why couldn't I stay with Auntie Wendy? (No offence, Marmaduke.) Why can't I forgive myself? Why can't I accept what has happened?

Marmaduke looks at me too. I almost shrug.

"Do you offer any… clubs or societies?" If John were here, he'd pull a face. Lame question.

She beams and lists the wonderful opportunities presented by her fine educational establishment.

"Any more questions?"

I shake my head. The meeting is mercifully over.

I don't like her because she looks like a vicious airhostess. Because her voice is annoying. Because she wears too much make-up. Because she has a slight moustache. Because she represents authority, and people in authority should always be distrusted. Because I'm 15 and I'd rather not go to school at all. But I tell my father that I'm looking forward to starting work again.

"I hated school," he says as we walk back to the apartment. He has rolled up his sleeves and unbuttoned his shirt a bit. "God, just being there brings back awful memories of being forced to play rugby in the winter and cricket in the summer when all I wanted to do was paint and sketch and be an artist. Actually, I think the Bohemian lifestyle appealed to me. I was going to ask her if sport is compulsory, but to be honest I didn't really feel like staying there much longer."

"How do you think I feel? I have to go there tomorrow."

"Granted, but you'll make friends and get into the whole thing."

"Didn't you have friends at school?" I ask.

"Oh, there were a few, I suppose. But nobody I'd call a soul mate or anything like that. I was very much a loner." He smiles. "Then I met your mother. She was a new pupil in our school in my final year, and we became best friends."

I didn't know they were at school together. Why didn't Mum tell me about that?

"Yes," Marmaduke says. "That's where I met her."

"She didn't tell me."

"Well, she probably had her reasons. Do you want to see a painting? No… not now… you probably need more time. I did a portrait of her just after we met. I still have it."

"So," I ask, knowing I'm leapfrogging the subject, "are you… famous?"

He laughs.

"I've developed a small following," he admits. "I've sold quite a few paintings and I'm starting to get more and more commissions, but I'm not world famous or anything. I have a… what you might call… an agent who exhibits and sells my work up on the mainland. And, thanks to Graham and Andrew, I have a small following here in the neighbourhood. Anyway, I earn enough to be able to devote all my time to it. Which reminds me, I'm going to be in the studio for the rest of the afternoon."

He gives me some money to buy things for school; but far too much, and tells me to enjoy my last day of freedom. I know exactly what I want to do.

Although there is a small aquarium on the island, it is not in Sandown. Sandown has a zoo containing, it proudly proclaims, a collection of tigers. But no dolphins. I want to see dolphins. I ask the woman at the ticket office whether she knows if there are dolphins at the aquarium and she tells me that the dolphinarium closed down many years ago, and no, there are no dolphins to be seen on the island.

Oh. Thanks. Now what?

I find that my fists are clenched as I walk back to the… no, I don't feel like going home. Neither do I feel like looking at a bunch of sad animals trapped in enclosures, away from their real homes. So instead I stand on the shore, glaring at the horizon. I feel like calling John, but I know he won't be home. I have called a few times since I arrived and it's always his mother who picks up the phone.

"Yes, I'll tell him you called. Yes, you gave me your number – I'll see that he gets it."

I know his mum. I know she has given him the message.

This is the part about being a teenager I don't like – this aimlessness, this feeling of not going anywhere, permanently looking for something to do. Because if I don't find something to do, I'll think too much, and if I think too much, I will go mad. Unless, of course, it's too late. Maybe these mood swings have nothing to do with being 15 and more to do with the slow descent into insanity. If things don't go my way, my mind is poisoned with evil thoughts of revenge, and I become so angry. And if I'm not angry, I'm moody, bored, or indifferent. I can go from happy to severely depressed in ten seconds, often without reason or prompting.

And sex – oh, God – up until Mum died… I was stripping people in my head, undressing them as they spoke. Sometimes I wondered if they knew what was on my mind. Wouldn't that be embarrassing? If we all had little screens on our foreheads, broadcasting our thoughts?

So Mum met Dad at school. If he left when I was five, and Mum died when she was 36 – my maths skills need sharpening – they must have been together for six years before they had me. Best friends for six years. Together for 11. Why did it take so long to end? Surely they would have known after a year or two that they had *irreconcilable differences*? And why couldn't they get along? Mum is, was, such a wonderful person; Marmaduke is very decent, very kind.

I don't understand.

Ugh, I say, when couples kiss on television. Mum just laughs.

It is neither warm enough to swim, nor hot enough to tan. I stand on the beach for a while, watching the sparkles on the water, listening to the waves. I know what I'll do.

But I can't. The tide is in; the rock pool is submerged. Shit.

I'm submerged again. Blue water surrounds me; the emptiness wraps its arms around me; holds me. I wait for the fish, and when the dolphin arrives, try to call out.

No sound, just bubbles.

Again the dolphin swims near me, but when I try to grab its fin, it darts off silently and disappears. I call out, waving my arms. Now I'm sinking, and the water is getting colder.

It is getting darker, although I see some sort of light far beneath me. The water is too cold; I don't like this – I want to breathe. Still I sink, faster and faster, until I realise that trying to swim upwards is dragging me down. I'm nearing the light. It is still very murky. Suddenly, my foot lands on something hard... something metal... a wreck of some sort? No – a car. I pull myself over until I can see into the vehicle. Strange that there are no... A woman is trapped behind the steering wheel. Her hair moves with the water; her eyes are wide open, her mouth frozen in a grimace, parts of her flesh bitten away by the fish I can't find.

YOU DID THIS, the woman shouts, and I shout and...

Marmaduke has his arms around me.

"Hush," he says in his gentle voice, "it's only a dream."

I'm sweating profusely. I can't stop shaking. I'm crying like a baby. The pain is unbearable.

"I keep seeing her stuck in the car," I manage to tell him. "Her face is..."

"Shh." He rocks me slowly. "I'm here. Everything's okay."

I don't want you to hold me like my mother did. It reminds me of her and makes things worse...

The morning light smacks me in the face as Marmaduke opens the curtains. "As much as I hate to do this," he says, "it's time for school. Breakfast will be ready soon. How are you feeling?"

"Like Monday," I say, and he laughs.

"I see you've already crossed out the days 'til the next holiday." He points to the calendar on my desk.

"I like thinking ahead," I reply.

I'm walking behind a boy and girl holding hands. They kiss each other as two boys race past, bumping school bags.

"I won!" one boy shouts when he reaches the corner.

I pass the beach-road shops and find a group of older boys trying to finish cigarettes quickly in an alleyway. Cars are beginning to congregate near the school gates. I'd be lying if I said I wasn't apprehensive. Nobody notices me, but I still sense threat lurking everywhere.

John and the others have got me cornered near the bike sheds and they are pounding me with their fists and their awful words. Even though I fight back, sort of, I am overwhelmed. Not least by John's betrayal.

I cross the street and enter through the school gates, trying not to look at anyone, trying to remember the way to that woman's office. I can imagine the scene: Hello, Christopher (smile), how are you? Isn't it a lovely day? Oh, I'm so pleased to see you. Okay, try not to look like the new kid. Be cool. Walk like you own the place. A few pupils at their lockers look at me, but I look away instantly.

Down the corridor, I walk past the artwork that Marmaduke had admired yesterday. There is a boy of my age waiting outside the office. He has surfer-blond hair and bright green eyes. When he sees me, he grins mischievously and nods.

"You Christopher?"

Girls from my other school would find him very attractive.

"Sometimes," I reply.

He's the kind of guy I wish I looked like.

"Me Tarzan." He extends his hand for me to shake. "Really. That's my surname. Tarzan. But you can call me James. And I probably won't answer because my name's actually Thane, short for Nathaniel, except I don't like to be called Nathaniel because I've got an uncle I can't stand. Damn, what happened to your head?" But before I can say anything, he adds, "See? I told you. If at first you don't succeed, skydiving's not for you... Anyway, welcome to our fine establishment. This is the Admin Block, or as we prefer, Cell Block H. Try, if at all possible, to stay away from here." He leans forward. "Sometimes kids get sent here and are never seen again."

This last bit is said with a deep voice, his eyebrows punctuating all insinuations.

"So where are you from?"

"London," I say, almost embarrassed that I am looking at him intently.

"Ah, London Town. You're lucky. All the clubs, all the music venues. We don't have much nightlife here. Beach parties mainly. And a big music festival. So which clubs did you go to?"

He has beautiful eyes.

I hastily try to remember names dropped by Auntie Wendy.

"Nah, don't know them," he says. "So why did you move?"

Do I, don't I?

Am I? Aren't I?

John's fists again.

"My dad's got a new job," I say, and make a point of looking at my surroundings.

"Oh. Cool. Welcome. And your head?"

"Swimming pool accident."

"That'll teach you. And they say swimming is a healthy pursuit. Now, down here we have No-Man's-Land. This," he points to the courtyard, "is where the bitches of the school hang out. You'll notice them soon enough. Wait 'til break. I call it No-Man's-Land because they're basically not worth it. Well, boys aren't welcome here, let me put it that way. And over here," he leads me through a corridor to the alcove and a garden, "is where the in-crowd tends to gather, so make your way here as soon as break starts."

The tour lasts ten minutes. I'm shown the science lab, the art room, the canteen, the assembly hall, the gymnasium, the language labs – and then the bell rings loudly, and my new life begins.

The teacher – Mr Edwards – has very red hair, a round, uncomplicated face, and lots of freckles. He smiles and extends a hand for me to shake.

"Class," he announces, "I'd like to introduce you to Mr Elliot, who joins us for the first time today."

I expect animosity, but no-one is leering. They look friendly enough.

"He's my friend," Thane replies, in a voice that sounds like he has conquered the world. "Treat him well; he's good people. The head's because of a swimming accident, so don't keep staring at it, it makes him self-conscious." Suddenly, 60 eyes beam in on my bruise. They are obviously used to Thane's antics, because they just smile and grin.

"Yes, Thane. So, welcome Chris. There's an empty seat next to Deirdre. Make him feel at home, Didi."

I make my way down the row to my seat, acknowledging Deirdre's smile. She's quite sweet-looking actually – a thin, angular face – confident features, brown hair.

I sit down as Mr Edwards adds, "You'll no doubt get to meet the others as the day progresses."

For some reason, I do not look around but stay focussed as he walks around the room distributing little slips of paper. Each contains an identity we have to assume when addressing the class. I'm interested in the activity greatly until I read what is written on my slip of paper.

BE YOURSELF.

"Okay," he says, turning to the class.

No, it's not okay.

"Right," he smiles at us. "So we're all on a flight overseas, and fire breaks out in all the engines. The plane is going to crash. But lo! Wouldn't you just know it, only one parachute. Well, what a conundrum! Thus, on the back of your slips of paper, I want you to jot down five reasons why you should get the parachute, bearing in mind that you are going to have to convince the class with not only your arguments but also your presentation and style."

"My name is…" The boy is tall, perhaps too tall for his age. He has a lock of dark hair that keeps getting into his eyes. He mentions a famous actor's name. "I should get the parachute because my fans won't be able to cope with my death. My music has been an inspiration across the generation's gaps." The class laughs. "I mean, my movies have been…"

Be yourself. Flipping hell. That's a tall order for my very first day. It would be easier if I actually knew myself who *yourself* is/was/is. There are so many people I would like to be. Some days I'm confident, I like myself – not vainly so – but on my terms. But other days I'm a whimpering little cry-baby. Then again, on others, if I want, I can be the friendly boy next door with a nothing-gets-him-down demeanour, or a rude, arrogant, stubborn brat who sulks if he can't get his own way. Do girls find me sexy?

Do boys?

Be yourself. Ho-hum.

"I'm SUPERMAN!" Thane proclaims. "But you can call me Kent. Clark Kent. People need to believe in me – you, even though you're all shortly going to die in a horrible inferno – you need to believe in me. You need to believe that somewhere in this crazy world of ours, there's someone who can solve national problems with a magnificent swoop of his cape. For I'm a symbol of hope, and hope should never be allowed to die."

Neither should mothers. Now who do we have to blame for that?

What on earth am I going to say? I practise in my head: Hi, I'm Chris. I think I should get the parachute because

1.   ???????
2.   ?????????????
3.   I don't deserve to get the chute. That's the truth. If you knew what I did…

As luck would have it, Thane is outstanding. I'm very envious of his confidence. But then he hasn't committed the crime I'm guilty of.

"Okay, Chris – you're next."

Shithellfirebrimstonecrap. I can try not to look at anyone in particular, although I know every eye is on me now.

"Um… as you know… my name's Chris…"

Duh. Remember to smile. Confidence.

"I… er… um…"

Oh, no!

"I think I should get the parachute… because… because… er…"

"Because," Thane chips in, "you are salt of the earth kinda people…"

No, I'm not.

"… and there isn't enough of that sort of person to go around anymore." He grins at me and holds up two thumbs.

"Thank you, Nathaniel," Mr Edwards replies.

Thane shoots his dirty hey-come-on look.

"Silly nana," someone says. Mr Edwards tells me to continue.

"Um…"

Who are you? Who are you? You deserve nothing.

"I don't want the parachute."

The others look bemused.

"But I would like to give it – if it were mine to give – to… to the woman with the child. Because I know she'd give it to the child. Er, thank you." To my relief I see appreciative nods and a few knowing smiles. From the girls.

"There we go," my teacher says. "Brief and concise, no

embellishments. Good. Very philanthropic."

I try to detect patronising inflections in his tone because I don't understand the long word. I don't find any.

"You'll get the sympathy vote because you're new," Deirdre whispers.

But I don't. The parachute goes to some foreign microbiologist who holds the formula to the cure for cancer. Typical. I'm hoping that I did not make a fool of myself. What do they think of me now? Will I be accepted into their little social circles, or are they going to treat me with distrust like I used to do to newcomers? Perhaps they think I'm a complete nerd or moron. Do I feel like a complete nerd or moron? Sometimes.

Often.

I meet up with Thane in the garden near the alcove. As I walk to the shade of a tree, I glance at the others. The in-crowd? They don't look particularly in-ish. They just look normal. Thane ruffles my hair, which doesn't irritate me at all.

"How was Science?" he asks.

I shrug.

"Science," I reply. "We were given homework."

"Bummer."

"So what makes these folk the in-crowd?" They just look like teenagers. Sloppy teenagers.

"We don't have any pretensions. And we don't wear labels. We're the kids who have opted out of the whole you-gotta-have-this-to-be-cool thing. You see, there are all sorts of little cliques around the school. Like…" he points to the corridor, where three boys with long black fringes lounge by the doorway, "The Lunatic Fringe. They seem – bless them – to want to keep the New Romantics tradition alive. Sad, but who can explain evolution? The Trendies parade around the pool. And if you go round the back to the fields, you'll find all the seniors on a little hill. Juniors aren't allowed up there."

"We're not juniors."

"We're in our second year of high school; you only become a senior in your fourth year."

"I hope it's worth the wait," I say, sitting down and leaning against the trunk of the tree.

"All the sporty types tend to stay out on the fields. Fun if you feel like exercise – there's always a game of something going on – noisy if you don't."

I ask him to tell me more about No-Man's-Land.

"What it is, you see, is most of the girls who have had their hearts broken and who now distrust and resent all males. Babes gone sour. Big time. And any male unfortunate enough to walk past is treated to a barrage of demeaning insinuation and downright insult. Most of us guys are trying to deal with puberty and acne. We don't have the mental skills to reply with suitable comedowns, or confidence. I know. I'm one of their victims. Vicious experience. Avoid at all costs." He grins, which is very appealing. "So whaddaya think of the place, Christof?"

I have no idea why he has taken such a shine to me, but I am so grateful for his company. I say, "It's a school."

That's right. He was told to look after me.

"Oh, no," he says, adopting a woman's voice, "it's a family." He looks at me quizzically. "Mrs Flank?"

I laugh. "Is she always so friendly?"

"Apparently," Thane moves closer, "she won some sort of Miss Congeniality Award when she was a teenager. Go figure. And she hasn't snapped out of it since."

"Oh," I say nodding, and for some very curious reason, I feel blissfully happy to have such an instant friend.

Oh, no, you're not allowed that.

Thane then pulls out a tennis ball, steps back and throws it high into the air. "Catch," he calls.

I catch it in one hand and hurl it up for him.

John and I are in his bedroom, play-fighting. And laughing. We're trying to emulate the wrestlers we have seen on television, but neither of us has the strength to do it properly. He is a bit stronger than I, and, at 12, getting hair in places I am not. He often brags about this, and as he pins me by the shoulders, I catch, for the first time, the smell of sweat on his body. His face is so close to mine I can feel his fringe against my forehead. I know his grip is not secure enough to keep me pinned, but, for a short while, I prefer being locked close together, almost tasting his breath.

The rest of the day passes without much incident. Thane is an engaging companion, who, I gather, speaks his mind without fear. To him, emotions are glass – transparent to anyone who cares to look. Fortunately, I'm not called upon to address any more classes, and, head down, I get on with the work. I don't want people to know what I'm feeling, what I'm about.

Thane doesn't seem to mind onlookers into his emotions. From what I can tell, he's quite popular. He jokes and fools around, but nobody seems to mind, and I get the feeling that among his peers, he is accepted because he is often funny, entertaining company.

At lunch break, a small crowd has gathered around me, firing questions, which I answer amiably and which I don't mind. They half-hear what I say, but when Thane speaks to imitate the school bully, they all listen. They laugh at what he says, but they are not laughing at him.

Homework done, I make my way down to the beach. Marmaduke is painting; I amble along the water's edge. It's warm enough to swim, so I do, which is fun, because I pretend to be a dolphin, enjoying the water.

After, while I'm drying, a few kids from school call my name and wave hello. I nod in return, but they don't come over. I carry my shoes in my hand to the rock pool, picking up shiny flat pebbles as I walk along.

"Well here we are once again, and I'm joined today by Chris Elliot, one of the sport of pebble hopping's bright young hopefuls. Chris, I understand you're one hop away from equalling the world record? How does it feel?"

"It feels great, Martin. I've never come this close before."

"Is today the day then? How confident are you that you will reach five hops?"

"It's hard to say. So many factors can influence the result: wind speed, the nature of the surface that changes every day. All I can say is, I'm going to try my best."

"Which is all your fans expect. You have quite a following for such a young player. How are you coping with the trappings of fame?"

I laugh.

"I'd love to chat, but I must get ready to start."

"Yes, folks, Chris Elliot's first attempt at equalling the world record. There's a hush among the crowd now as he selects his stone. He holds it up for the judges to approve. They do, and he steps forward. Mike, what are your thoughts on the condition of the surface of the water?"

"It's not as smooth as the last time; there's a bit of a ripple, which might drag the stone a bit, but this youngster looks undeterred. He really is something else, this young man. Confident, and at the same time almost mysterious. Wouldn't you say, Deirdre?"

"Oh, of course, Mike. I think that's definitely part of his allure. We ladies like that in a budding champion. Back to you, Martin."

"Thank you, Deirdre. The tension is rising as Chris Elliot, the coastal contender, prepares for throw number one. He's up against some tough opposition, though. Nathaniel Conrad has also qualified for today's heat. He's waiting by for his turn."

Mustn't think of the others. Must stay focussed.

"And look at that stone go — an almost perfect release there — it's hopped once, twice, three times… oh, it's just run out of momentum.

There's a collective sigh of disappointment. Chris is not happy about that throw at all. He shakes his head. It looks like he's muttering to himself.

Thane steps forward, displays his chosen stone. The crowd has gone silent now. Notice the absolute concentration, folks. He's thrown it; what a superb slicing action. Once! Twice! Three… four times! Well, if that isn't throwing down the gauntlet, I don't know what is.

The pressure is on Chris Elliot. Actually, I must say, Chris is looking very determined. He's rolling his pebble in his palm, looking seriously at the surface.

Here he goes. Once… twice… three… four… ah, only four. Well, he'll be more pleased with that attempt. Four hops apiece. Join us after the break for round two of this remarkable tournament."

A man and a fishing rod walk by. I must make sure I'm not speaking aloud. I wait for him to pass.

"We're back, and we've just heard that Nathaniel Conrad has thrown his second pebble, but it hit the water and sank after one, which gives Chris Elliot the break he was hoping for."

COASTAL CONTENDER
QUIETENS CRITICS

Chris Elliot, a relative new-comer to the sport of pebble hopping, amazed the critics today when his pebble hopped five times at the amateur pebble hopping championships held this evening.

Chris now goes through to the next round, where he'll meet reigning title holder and all-time favourite, Dodge Johnson – and what a clash that promises to be.

Back at the apartment, Marmaduke emerges from his studio when he hears the door slam. For a moment, I think he is angry I hadn't closed the door more gently, but he's smiling.

"I've ordered pizza for tonight."

"Excellent."

I'm about to go into my room when he says, "I have something for you." He pops back into the studio and comes out with a small canvas, slightly larger than A4. He turns it around. It's a portrait of Mum when she was a schoolgirl. He has captured the naughty glint in her eyes. My eyes immediately well up, but I keep control.

"This is how she looked when I first met her. I want you to have this. I want you to try and remember this image of her to keep the nightmares at bay."

The nightmares. I try to ignore them during the day. I try not to think about them at all.

It's a beautiful painting: very realistic portrait; quite abstract background. She is staring up at what looks like the moon, but it's too large – it must be a planet. She is bathed in soft light; her eyes mischievous, her smile so simple and sincere.

"It's lovely," I say, hoping my voice doesn't betray emotion. "Where do you want me to hang it?"

"Oh," he replies, shrugging, "it's yours. You'll find a place to hang it when the time's right."

Later, in the sitting room, he says, "I painted that three months after meeting Sarah."

"When did you first realise you were in love?" I ask, stretching out on the couch. He pours a Coke and passes the glass to me.

"Cheers."

He sips his drink and leans back. He smiles.

"The moment we met," he says, and I'm touched by the tenderness in his voice.

"She was a cocky little thing. Do you know, when she first arrived in my class, she demanded that she sit in my seat, which was next to the window. Not asking. Demanding."

"Did you offer her your seat?"

"God, I would have offered her the world. She was so radiant, so direct. How could I resist? I remember thinking, when the teacher asked her to explain some maths answer, and she said, "Maths has nothing to do with love, and love is all that matters to me," – I remember thinking, she's such a challenge. Difficult, demanding, awfully forthright in her dealings with the world. Oh, she was captivating. But we didn't actually hit it off right away. I didn't want her to know… how I felt, so I was very stroppy and acted unimpressed. "I'm going to make you my friend just to spite you," she told me. I used to like painting alone in the art studio at school during breaks, but she followed me in there and harassed me with all sorts of unbelievably personal questions." He laughs.

I like listening to him. It hurts to hear about Mum, but it's something I need to hear. I know he is talking about my mother, but the glaze in his eyes suggests someone far more important. Did they really love each other? Why did they split up? I decide not to ask these questions because I don't think this is the right moment.

"But as far as getting together romantically is concerned, well, that only happened about a year after that. We had a kind of love-hate relationship, which became a friendship. We were at a party one night, and I saw her being chatted up by other guys and the confident way she flirted with everyone. I realised I liked her because she seemed so independent. So secure in her views and how she expected the world to treat her. But the odd thing is, in the beginning I had the impression that she was the one chasing after me, but as soon as I took the bait and told her how I felt, she became aloof and standoffish. I suppose I over-romanticised love, and she wanted none of that. Love was matter of fact, shut-up-and-accept-it, don't screw around with feelings, grit and grime reality. She detested soppy romanticism, which she said was rife in my paintings, and did not want that to be the motivation for having a relationship. She wanted me to love her for who she was, so she let me see the warts and all, so to speak. 'Love has pimples,' she used to say."

As he speaks, I try to deflect the gnawing reminder that she would still be alive today if…

We talk until late in the night; or rather, he talks, I just listen. I don't mind. He's not just my father; he was once a teenager like me. He recalls many an anecdote and seems to get pleasure from sharing them. For the first time, I get a glimpse into how he felt for her. That he loved her is obvious. That he still does… well, I think so. He talks about her with such tenderness. I realise now that he is grieving for more than just the past.

When I go to bed, I stare at her portrait. There is no condemnation, no accusation in her eyes.

There should be.

There is a knock on my bedroom door. I open my eyes and see Thane. It's six o'clock in the morning. Friday morning. He apologises to Marmaduke once again, and I hear Dad say that he was up anyway.

"Get up you lazy piece of vermin trash," Thane announces cheerfully. He opens the curtain to allow in the quiet light of the morning.

"Up you get." He sits on the edge of my bed. "Jeez – no wonder you're single – look at you in the morning." His grin is cheeky.

"What are you doing here?" I manage to ask grumpily. "It's so early. It's too early."

"I've come to show you something."

"Where? What?"

"Get up. Get dressed. Come alive with Radio Five. Hurry up."

He's come to show me – I don't believe this – the beach in the morning. I live so near the damn place, and I know what it looks like, but he wants to sit on the sand watching the sunrise.

"I like that it is a new day. A new beginning," he says with a smile.

And now here I am, out in the morning air, munching apples while listening to the sound of the waves. It's a cloudless start. Thane offers hot chocolate from a flask. We watch birds peck at seaweed.

"I don't usually get up this early," he admits, "but I thought that today was a good day to get back to basics and enjoy the simple things in life." He stands up and lets the wind blow the sand from his hand.

"Simple things like sleeping," I suggest.

"Nah, what do you want to be in bed for? It's much nicer out here." He wanders off towards the water's edge and stands facing the horizon with his hands in his pockets.

"Best time of the day this," I hear him say. "Isn't it beautiful?" Then he runs and does a cartwheel, then a forward somersault. "I flipping love this time of day!" he shouts. When he returns, he playfully kicks sand in my direction.

"Sod off!" I reply, chucking a handful at him.

"Do your parents ever argue?" he asks suddenly, sitting down.

I take a while before answering. "No," I say. "I've never heard them fight."

"Mine do," he turns to look at the horizon. "Sometimes as early as five in the flipping morning." He shakes his head. "He shouts and she shouts as soon as they get up. That's all they ever do. Flipping amazing. It's been weeks since they've said anything civil to each other."

A part of me wants to put my arms around him for comfort, but by his tone I can tell he's not looking for sympathy.

And after what happened with John… no, best I don't.

So that's why we're here. He needed to get out of the house.

"They've been at each other a lot lately. I don't know why they bother really. It would be much better if they were apart. There'd be less damage done. Hey, guess what? Deirdre fancies you."

"She doesn't."

"She does, I heard it from Ellie – and she should know." He smiles. "So? What are you going to do about it?"

"Nothing. Yet."

"Ah, so you like her?"

"Stop fishing. I like no-one." This is almost true, but...

"Yeah, sure. I saw the way you were looking at her."

I shake my head. I'm flattered if it's true, but as I said, not now.

"So why aren't you involved?" I ask.

He grins. "With the role models I've got? Get real."

He is right about one thing, though. It is beautiful out here at this time of day.

He is not as bubbly as he was yesterday, and at school he's not afraid to tell others why. That surprises me. The way he can tell everyone his problems without it sounding like a plea for sympathy. And as for Deirdre, now that Thane's spilled the beans, I feel really uncomfortable around her. It's not that she's not attractive – she is – but the reason I'd want to go out with her would be because it might improve my social status at the school, and I don't think that's reason enough. See? I can be honest with myself. At break, Thane mentions something about a party tomorrow night.

"Anything to get out of the house. You're coming too of course."

"I haven't been invited."

"You have now."

I shake my head.

"I don't think so."

"Crap. I need you to be there. You're my friend now, so you're obligated. I know it's tough, but that's how it plays, I'm afraid."

Auntie Wendy sounds different, excited.

"Ooh, I've a filthy secret to confess. You'll never guess."

She's right.

"I met someone," she whispers.

"So?" I reply. "I meet new people every day."

"Someone very dashing, very well-groomed."

"Probably gay," I say, without having a clue why.

"That's what I thought at first. But no – he's the last of a dying breed of gentlemen."

"In other words, he's old and will croak soon?"

"No, you daft fart. He's two years older than I. And he thinks I'm

72

wonderful."

"I think you're wonderful. How come you're not with me?"

"Because someone else is reserved for you."

"Who?"

"That's for you to find out. And you will. You'll see."

"Yeah, right. If you say so. So when do I get to meet this Mr Wonderful? You know you can't do anything until he gets my approval. I have high standards, you know."

"Yes, well I don't, and it's too late."

"You didn't."

A giggle.

"Auntie Wendy, you didn't…"

"I couldn't help myself. He's gorgeous."

"Strumpet," I call her, and she laughs.

A woman and her son are driving along the motorway. The mother has just turned down the volume on the car's cassette deck.

"But Mum…" the boy whines.

"Not too loud," she says.

Then, like a naughty little child, he surreptitiously slides his arm over to the volume dial.

"I'll thump you," his mother says.

CHAMPION UNABLE TO BREAK OWN RECORD

Chris Elliot, reigning pebble champion, failed today in his bid to beat his own record of five hops. "It's still a challenge, so I'll keep trying," he told reporters this afternoon. "I want to be the first to reach six or maybe even seven hops. If it's possible, I'll do it. I don't know when – soon I hope – but I'll do it."

The WonderBabe

Thane, I'm beginning to realise, is a master of mimicry, and he is running through his entire repertoire in an attempt to convince me to go to the party tonight. He's done Mrs Flank; Gregory, the school wimp (he cries whenever he has to do basically anything); Tron, the school Dinner Lady; and…

"Alright you stupid little shit." He advances with a swagger, his mouth curled nastily. He opens his mouth to continue, but it takes a while for any ideas to catch up.

"John Wayne?"

"You," he snarls, grabbing my throat. "Don't think you can mess with ME. I WILL see you at the party tonight."

"Mr Ellis?"

"Mr Ellis?"

"Yeah, he was my history teacher when I was 12."

"How the flip am I supposed to know him? You're cheating." He sulks.

"How can I be cheating? It's your game. Oliver Twist."

"The only thing twisted around here is your mind, boy. But I can do Oliver." He approaches with his best Victorian orphan expression. "Please, Sir – come to the party tonight."

"Nah."

"Nah my impersonation sucks? Or nah you're not coming?"

"I told you, I don't want to go."

"But why? It's not normal at your age to refuse party invitations. There must be a reason. Is it your old man?"

I could tell him. I could just open my mouth and tell him.

I could.

It is Saturday morning. Thane has popped over to do stuff. I think he's bored at home. We are in my kitchen, it is ten o'clock, and Marmaduke is in his studio. Thane insists that I go to this party. It's at some girl called Jenny's house. She's a senior but her brother knows Thane, so it's cool if we go.

"It's not my father," I say. I know I'm not going to tell him the real reason. I don't know if I will ever tell him or anybody ever. Our friendship is still quite new, and although I really don't mind his company at all, there are things I don't wish to tell him.

"Is it your mother? Where is she by the way? I'm making toast. Do you want some?"

"She's away on business. What are you going to put on it?"

"I dunno. What've you got?"

"Look in the cupboard."

"So?" he says, searching for something to spread on the toast. "So why don't you want to come?" He opens the fridge. "Choccie Spread! Bingo!"

"I don't like parties."

That's not true. I know that's not true. I'm a teenager.

"Bing! Wrong. You'll have to try harder. Crap excuse."

"I don't like crowds?"

He looks at me. "Oh, please." He says it like Auntie Wendy would when she disbelieves one of my stories. "You're weird. There'll be alcohol, there'll be drugs, there'll be girls." Then his voice changes. "Lots of really really loverly gihirls."

"Not my scene."

"You're into boys?" He recoils and grins. He looks at me expectantly. My expression stays the same.

"The party scene. Not my scene."

Liar, liar, liar.

"It's God, isn't it? God's done this to you. I've seen it happen before. You're not going because you are not allowed to go." Then he adds, "But you're not religious, are you?"

"Why don't you just stop hassling me about this party?" I don't say this with any malice.

"Because it don't make sense, man. It don't make sense."

Like the phone call to John last night.

He was home, finally. But he wasn't, metaphorically. It was like talking to a stranger. I was talking to a stranger. He seemed at a loss for words, and there were long gaps of uncomfortable silence and an almost irritated edge to his tone. He sounded… reluctant, as if the call was compulsory, and now some sort of contact had been made, he wanted to get it over with. Each question was forced, and even though I did my best to sound cheerful, I too wanted to end the conversation, if only because it was getting me down.

We used to be such good friends.

It appears he has a completely new life; another completely new girlfriend. Is it because he is uncomfortable with my mother's death? I read somewhere that people don't know how to relate to people who grieve. Or maybe it is simply because we have grown apart as friends?

Or maybe he knows…?

I'm uncertain how I feel about this. Everything is my fault.

Accept responsibility. Be a man.

If I think too much, the feeling is like a child coming inside to play but finding the front door locked and his parents have moved. Another part of me is too scared to feel sorrow at the distance between us – John and me – because it might cause the other balloons to burst. Like a chain reaction. I feel like I'm beginning to have more control over the floodgates, and I don't want to lose that feeling. The only thing that matters now is not losing control, not turning into Gregory the wimp. If I can try not to feel anything too intense, then I can hold on, I can cope, I won't have to feel the pain. Maybe that's how Auntie Wendy gets through? By rationalising everything, she neutralises the urge to rage at life's crueller side.

Thane has gone off to play volleyball on the beach. I don't feel like being all sporty and active today. I just want to lounge about and read comics and watch TV. I could go to the zoo of course, but I'm not in the mood. I'm bored. I could start thinking about painting my room, but that seems like work. I could start thinking about my biology project. Miss Alwyn gave out a list of possible study topics and told us to choose, except that we each had to choose a different area of study and I ended up with BOTANY: Investigate a plant.

That's it. That's my topic. I know I said I wanted my life to be free of extremes, but… Thane gets to study up on sharks, Dean on infectious diseases, Karen on the paranormal powers of animals, and by the time the list came to me, all that was left was BOTANY: Investigate a plant.

Detective Chris Elliot checks his watch and grimaces. Rarely has he seen a crime scene so gruesome. Phrases like "the root of all evil" and "the FBI branch" stand poised to bungee jump from his mouth. Only one thing could be responsible, Chris thinks to himself, for such carnage. Harry the Hibiscus. Chris imagines the reporters rushing to get the story and rehearses his bit. "Yeah, I knew it was Harry alright. I twigged the second I walked into the room."

Marmaduke is in his studio. He came out a little while ago to fetch water and told me he has started working on a project commissioned by a large firm in Portsmouth. He's been busy the last few days.

The programmes on television are boring, and I've got no new books to read. That's not entirely true. Marmaduke has a collection – mainly artists' biographies – but I don't feel like reading anything serious. I usually read detective stories or crime novels, mysteries, or war books.

It's eight o'clock. Thane will be getting ready to go to the party now. A huge part of me wishes I was there, if only to spend some time with him. My new friend. Him.

What does that mean?

I know what it doesn't mean.

I don't want to go to the party because seeing other people's happy lives makes me feel uncomfortable. It's pathetic, I know.

I don't want to go to the party because… because I do not trust myself. There. You happy, Chris? Kris? Christ.

I don't like being 15.

If, as some people believe, the spirits of the departed are watching over us, do they look away when we masturbate or go to the toilet? I wonder about this because… I wonder if I should go to my room… because nothing.

I reach for the TV guide.

I'm bored, and, if I am honest with myself, a little lonely.

"What's up?" Marmaduke asks. I didn't hear him enter the sitting room. "Oh, sorry. Did I wake you?"

"What's the time?" I'm on the couch with the TV turned down.

"About eleven, I think."

"Then you have woken me. You finished your work?"

"Yes. Did you sort out something to eat? I'm sorry I didn't make supper."

"I finished off last night's stew."

"Oh, good."

When I ask him how he manages to stay focussed for so long on his work, he says, "Because it doesn't feel like work. The time passes by very quickly."

"It's not because you're trying to ignore me?"

It's a flippant, nonsensical remark, which spreads alarm all over his face.

"Oh, I'm so sorry, Kris," he says. "I... I don't want to hijack your weekends. It's... er... this commission. It's... it's very important because it has the potential to open other doors."

"It's okay," I say. "I'm only kidding. Seriously."

I don't know how, but we end up talking about Mum again. Again he goes to the studio to fetch something he's painted while courting her. I'm not familiar with the term, and he laughs when I tell him.

"Because your mother... Sarah had such a thing about soppy romance, when I realised that what I felt for her was genuine, I decided to piss her off by courting and wooing her quite openly. For instance, she threw a bucket of water over me when I sang beneath her bedroom window once. I used to send her roses regularly, attached to really soppy poems – deliberately soppy poems, and her mother told me she used to eat them." He sees the look of incredulity on my face. "The roses. Really. She ate them in a salad."

I've noticed that Marmaduke is trying very hard to make me feel at home, and sometimes when he speaks, it sounds like he is aware of what his words might make me feel.

Be honest. You know that things will never be the same. But they could also be a lot worse.

Yet, when he talks about Mum or his paintings, he is not aware of me at all. It's like he's talking to himself, and he doesn't mind that

I'm listening. He explains why his *Still Life of Roses with Teeth Marks* is one of his favourites. The roses are in a vase on a plate next to a spoon. It's amazing what you see when you know what to look for.

I realise that, like *Magic Eye* pictures, if you know how to look, you see more than you expect. In the glass vase is the faint reflection of a girl; the figure is barely recognisable, but it's there, gently expressed, like a whisper. Behind the table, a sign says, "You are what you eat." He told me that Mum thought it wasn't subtle enough and that she always criticised his work ruthlessly. "How else will you get better?" she asked.

The telephone rings. Marmaduke answers and says it's Thane.

Be still…

It's also twelve thirty and way too late to call. Yet Marmaduke doesn't seem to mind. Thane sounds drunk. He wants me to meet him on the beach. Marmaduke says I can go.

So late at night? Why does he want to see me unless… ah, that's why… his folks are probably fighting again.

It's funny. As I cross the road and make my way to the sand, I feel sad to leave Marmaduke alone.

Thane is not as drunk as he sounded on the phone. He swaggers when he greets me. "I don't… feel like… going home yet," he says almost as an apology. He's wearing an earring. I never noticed that before.

Remember what Mum said: if you want to keep a friend, be a friend.

"How was the party?"

"You missed nothing." He gesticulates loosely. "It was… you missed nothing. As dull as a wart on a pensioner's nose. Deirdre was there. She asked after you. I told her you thought she was cute."

The waves sound louder late at night.

"You didn't."

"I didn't. I was going to, though. But common sense prevailed. Shit, I hate it when that happens." My relief is visible, and he grins. "But I drank, so maybe I did tell her and just can't remember. Who can tell?"

"If you have," I threaten, not knowing what to threaten him with, "I'll…"

"Relax. Your secret's safe with me."

What secret?

"What secret?"

"I know you like her."

"Bullshit, shithead."

"Ooh."

"If you told her anything remotely to do with romance and me, I will tell Mrs Flank that you... that you fantasise about her." Lame, but it's late.

"All the seniors stuck together in little groups and the only person I could talk to was David, but he went off with some girl. Lucky shit. I wanted to leave sooner, but..." He shakes his head. Then he sighs, and shrugs. "Things at home are really crap nowadays."

I don't know what to say.

"Fantasise about her?" he says. "I don't think so. I wonder how far they got, David and that girl? Have you ever slept with anyone?" The question takes me by surprise.

Have you ever swum naked underwater?

What do I tell him? He'd probably know I am lying.

"Nah. Not even close. You?"

The million-dollar question.

"Once, almost."

Nathaniel and the girl hold hands while walking on the beach in the moonlight. Violins can probably be heard in the background. He pulls her to him and leans forward. Their lips meet.

"Did Deirdre end up with someone?"

He grins again. "Why do you want to know?"

"I don't. Did she?"

"No, she left early. Her folks are quite conservative, I think. What did you do all evening?"

"Nothing." Which is true.

We sit and watch the light of the moon, scattered on the water.

"Hey," I ask, "what are these wooden fences along the beach? These ones that stretch into the water?" I have noticed them before, but never wondered what they were actually for or called.

"Groynes," he replies.

"You're kidding me."

"Not groins, dipshit. G-R-O-Y-N-E-S. They're to stop beach erosion."

It's too late. I am thinking of his groin.

"So when's your mum coming back?" he asks after a while. "You don't talk about her much. She's away on business, right? Isn't that what you said?"

If I say one word about her, I will cry and never be able to stop. If I talk about what happened with anyone except Auntie Wendy, I will implode. So I reply, "What's to say? She's a mother. Aren't all mothers alike?"

You must know you can't keep quiet forever? Sooner or later...

I'm sorry, Mum. Not now. Just... not now.

"Mine's a..." He pauses and looks serious. "You know, when they're not fighting, you can still feel the tension in the house. It's like something you can almost touch. I'm too scared to open my mouth in case one of them snaps at me, because basically when they're tired of taking it out on each other, there's only one other person to take it out on. Don't you wish you had brothers and sisters?"

Always. But I also wish I had a friend who wanted only me.

It's odd how he intersperses extremely personal comments with loose, casual talk. If he wants to talk about his parents, why doesn't he just let it all out instead of dropping them into the conversation and then changing the subject? Images of pots and kettles go whirring around my mind. He doesn't usually have trouble talking about his feelings.

"Not really," I say. "I like being an only child. Sometimes I wish I had a brother, but most of the time I don't." I want to tell him about Mum, but he needs someone to listen, I think. "What's going on at home?"

The sound of the waves.

He looks up at the moon.

"Why do two people stay together when they are quite obviously not meant to stay together?" He sighs. "I don't understand them, Chris. I don't know why they hate each other so much. Sometimes I think it's my fault."

I reach out for his arm, but end up pushing him slightly.

"It's not your fault."

"How do you know? You should hear them. I don't think they've spoken softly to each other in months. Parents. Go figure." He gets up and walks towards the water's edge. "Do you feel like swimming?" he calls, taking off his shirt. "Come for a dip."

"My trunks are at home," I say, ambling over.

"So?" he replies. "We're both boys and we're not queer, so who needs to wear anything?"

"It's late and it's not that warm," I say feebly. "Some other time. Chuck me your stuff. I'll look after it."

I sit down, because if I stay standing up, everyone will know that I am standing up. He peers at me quizzically and shakes his head.

"You don't want to go to parties. You don't wanna swim…" He shrugs. "Suit yourself, wimp."

He smiles, removes his jeans and runs into the water. He does not take off his boxer shorts. He squeals at the cold. If it were me, I would have gone in slowly, but he runs in and dives under the swell, emerging with a "Flipping heck!" as he turns to face me. He is better built than I am, with more muscular arms, and for a moment, again, I wish I could look like him.

"Come on!" he shouts. "It's flipping freezing!"

"Be careful of the sharks!" I shout back.

The water's so cold…

"Come on, Chris!" He turns and dives, seal-like, into an oncoming breaker, and emerges whooping on the other side. Then he is engulfed by a wave and emerges spluttering. Now I am up, taking off my trousers, but, like him, not my Y-fronts. And I run into the water. And I run straight back out. And not because it is cold, though that's the excuse I give.

Shit.

He returns soon. He is shivering. He uses his T-shirt to dry himself, puts his jeans back on and then his shirt. I offer him my jersey because it'll warm him up, but he says never mind.

"What's the time?"

When I tell him, he says, "Shit. I've gotta go home soon. My old man will knock seven kinds of shit out of me if I'm late."

"Yeah, I guess I should go home too. You want some hot

chocolate?"

He says, shaking his head, "I'm already a bit late as it is. My old man will slaughter me."

"If you don't… if you need somewhere to crash tonight, you can doss over at my place."

"No, thanks. I'll be fine. But I'll take you up on that offer of a jersey, if you don't mind."

I walk with him to the corner of my road. And that's how I leave him, wearing Mum's jersey, running at the moon.

I'm falling. Jesus, I am falling. I expect to land with a thud but hear a splash. The water is so cold. I call out for my mother. She must be here knitting somewhere. I call and I call and soon my mouth is filled with seawater. I try and try and try and try to stay afloat, but my jumper and jeans are weighing me down. I tear at them while sinking, and even when they drift away, like washing in a watery wind, I am still sinking.

Shouting underwater.

Why am I still alive? I can't see anything and feel only panic. It seems the more I try to get to the surface, the deeper I go and the darker it gets.

Something slimy grabs me by the ankle, and snake-like, curls itself around my legs. It's someone's arm.

I scream and I scream and I scream.

Marmaduke is holding me tightly. His shirt is drenched. I cry myself back to sleep.

Music. Pop music. A party. Everyone is having fun. It's a fantastic evening, and I am drunk.

"I am too," says John, and we giggle like schoolgirls, which makes us laugh even more. He has his arm around me, more to keep himself steady than anything else. We stumble, falling over each other, and giggle more. The moon does a jig in the sky. When we sit up, we find ourselves alone.

"Where is everybody?" he calls, and then, like a lost little child, he says, "They're all gone." He falls back and repeats "They're all gone," closing his eyes. "But you're here," he mumbles.

Soon he is asleep, and I cannot stop staring at him. At his body. He is a good friend. One of the best. One in a million. Oh, John. Oh, John. You're my best friend. This is all a dream. The only word to describe you is beautiful. I stare and stare at him. I can't help myself. My hand, snake-like, makes its way to the button of his jeans.

"What are you doing?" he shouts. "What do you think you're doing?"

But I won't let him go. I grab him by the shoulders... and kiss... Thane.

I've done my homework. The rest of Sunday stretches before me without much invitation. I swim in the pool for a while, until some of the other residents with their children come down to tan. Not play swimming – proper lengths and strokes. I don't pretend to be a dolphin or a diver seeking treasure or anything like that. I've decided I'm too skinny and I need to tone up. I've also decided that this does not have to be a lengthy sentence. If I don't feel like doing it tomorrow, I won't. It's just today I feel like trying it out. My neighbour's kids are loud and splash about a lot, bombing each other with spray.

I could go swimming at the beach, but by now it has filled up substantially; I can see the masses and I don't feel like crowds. I can, I know, take a walk further up the coast where there are fewer people. The idea takes hold and I scribble a message for Marmaduke before leaving the apartment.

There are a lot of couples on the beach. The smell of tanning oils hits me as I weave through the sun-thirsty throng, ducking Frisbees and avoiding dogs and games of catch ball. Soon I'm able to walk along the water's edge with my jeans rolled up and there are fewer and fewer people to pass. The sand is fringed by loose vegetation, the little slopes hugging the road get bigger, and the road drifts higher and away from the sand to where it hugs the hill giving rise to the cliff. There is a faint mist ahead, despite the sun. A few men are fishing. I have to think about what I'm going to do for my biology project. Perhaps I should ask Auntie Wendy? It's a thought. She likes plants and stuff. So did...

"A Bond's Eye," Mum says. "Christopher, it's beautiful." She holds the miniature tree gently and smiles. "This would make the perfect gift for some lucky woman."

We are at the nursery to get plants for her room. It's her birthday in three days. I take the hint. Which is not the same as actually remembering her birthday; I don't, and get her a box of chocolates instead.

The sound of the waves.

I wonder if she can see me now? It's been a few weeks. Do spirits only linger for a short while afterwards…? Before what? What happens next? If there's a heaven, is she in it? If there's a hell…?

A part of me still wishes the phone will ring and Mum will be on the other end, telling me there has been a huge misunderstanding, that she's forgiven me and is coming to take me home.

God, how I wish that were so.

I like the feel of the sun on my skin. I like walking here and being on my own. I like living here and having Thane as a friend. I like that not many people know me here – not many people know – but I don't like the fact that I will never see my mother again. So by all accounts, I should be happy. Except for… Here I go again, I'm thinking too much.

I've found some really cool pebbles – really smooth; just the right size.

So Auntie Wendy has a boyfriend. So Deirdre likes me, apparently. At school yesterday I couldn't quite tell. She just seemed her usual friendly self, although I did catch her smiling at me. I've told you she's pretty. Have I told you that I don't want to ask her out because it would complicate my life terribly? I can afford to ask girls out now, but I cannot afford the burden of a relationship. Maybe all this is mere conjecture. Maybe she likes someone else.

Why am I even thinking about her?

I like girls. I so do.

Up ahead, the sand stops and the rocks become boulders as the coast turns inwards and becomes a rocky cliff. The road is high above me. Waves smash the shore here, sending up huge explosions of spray. I think I'll hold the interview on that rock over there.

"Mr Elliot, may I call you Chris?"

"You may."

"Well, here you are, literally basking in the glory of being a world champion. And I wonder, did you ever dream that one day you would reach the heights that you have?"

"I don't think I've reached the heights I would like to. I'll need to take the record to seven hops before I can feel I've achieved my potential."

I hear the sound of a car screeching as it skids along the coastal road. I don't know why, but I expect to see it flying through the air, crashing on the rocks below. It doesn't, but there's an awful moment when I'm sure it is going to. When, just for a second, I hear echoes from the past and I almost remember the moment of impact. But the car on the road above is safe: no barricades are broken, no car plummets to the bottom. Perhaps the driver in a split second turned the wheel the right way and avoided a tragedy. That is what is meant by a fine line between life and death: just a fraction of a second can make the difference between being hit by a stray bullet and bending down to tie your shoelaces. I remember the day I met John and how I pretended to shoot him with an invisible gun. I remember that second before I pulled the invisible trigger. I remember one night, the second before I kissed him, and the second after, when everything changed. It is disturbing to think how much depends on the smallest fraction of time. Weird thoughts, these.

A woman and her son are driving along the motorway. Their tyre bursts and they crash into a pole. But the second before that...

I think I'll join the others on the beach. I'm a teenager. I'm allowed to be fickle.

Thane is waiting by the school gates with a bright, cheerful smile. Not a Mrs Flank kind of smile, but his own guess-what-I've-just-done smile. I'm pleased to see him looking cheerful. Maybe things are better at home. I'm pleased to see him because I had another dream about vicious dolphins last night. *Don't think about it now; don't let it ruin your day.* Once again Marmaduke was there to tell me it was just a dream. My spirits are immediately lifted when Thane says, "You're looking nicely tanned."

We start the day with Biology, and we are going to be asked about our projects. I lied: I haven't done all my homework. I tried to phone

Auntie Wendy but she was out. I almost phoned John, but that would have been silly.

Miss Alywn asks each of us, in turn, to stand and describe our proposals. My mind races for... oh, dammit, I should have thought of this last night. Thane announces that he intends studying the great white; we can look forward to a graphic display of gory details. Everyone else has ideas that are fresh and far more exciting than my idea, which is... plants. Come on... investigate which plant? What kind of plant? Um. Names of plants. Roses, tulips – no, those are flowers.

"Chris?"

I have to stand up. I do.

"Rhododendrons."

I've no idea what they are but that's what I tell the class I'm going to investigate. Miss smiles. I can sit down without feeling embarrassed, without Miss having to be displeased. I don't want to draw that kind of attention to myself.

Mr Phillips is an unusual history teacher. He has a way of seeing history in context, and when he speaks about past events, it's as if he were really there. Today he warns us about a video of the Nazi concentration camps and even offers to wait behind after class if anyone needs to talk about what they have seen. It doesn't bother me, because I enjoy war books. I have read loads.

The preamble whets our appetites, but before he pulls down the blinds, he walks forward, and, lowering his voice, says, "You're not going to be able to look at this without it hitting you quite hard. There is no reasonable explanation for the things you will witness today; no explanation for the sheer cruelty and barbaric inhumanity of war. This really happened. What you are about to see is not a Hollywood blockbuster, and nor does it contain actors or special effects. My only fear is that there might be some amongst you who are, for various reasons – arcade games and videos being to blame – immune to the horror of what really happened. I hope I am proved wrong."

Horror is a word that is inadequate to describe the images we see. The bodies, tossed like garbage, piled upon each other, the endless grey gore. Watching it makes me feel numb. Even though I have read about it, and thought about it, I am not prepared to actually see it. The usual peanut-gallery comments are absent. The narrator's voice is impassioned and I wonder how anyone can remain so calm. It's a grizzly lesson, and it affects us all. The discussion that follows focuses on why people can allow one another to be treated that way. It then moves on to a query about why God allows such things to happen, and while the others heartily participate, I feel the balloon inside begin to inflate and I have to bite my lip.

Mum and I grapple over the volume switch and, because of me, she removes her hands from the wheel.

I can't think about this now. I simply can't. I have to put it out of my head. I have to.

I can't help but think, as I make my way to Maths – aargh – about the nature of evil, and how evil things happen, and how, sometimes, it can be created from the most innocent sources. I pass a poster, which says:

WE ARE ALL GIVEN A DREAM, AND WITH IT, THE
POWER TO MAKE IT COME TRUE.
Certainly true in Mr Hitler's case.
YOU MAY HAVE TO WORK FOR IT, HOWEVER.
I didn't notice that bit at first. Someone should have added,
AND WHEN YOU GET IT, LIFE WILL DEMAND IT
BACK. WE ARE NEVER GIVEN HAPPINESS; IT ALWAYS
DRIFTS AWAY.

Like I said, weird thoughts.

You know I said that so much could depend on a split second? Well, get this: as I walk into the maths class, I accidentally bump into another boy who has already started shaving but hasn't today. Accidentally. I don't see him behind the door. It's not my fault. But he glares at me with such hatred, and he won't accept my apology.

"Just you wait," he growls, before taking his seat. For the rest of the lesson, if he sees me looking at him, which I cannot help but do, he grimaces. Just why this should scare me, I don't know. For some reason, I find myself hoping that the few lengths I did yesterday had pumped me up enough to survive a fight. Now, the fact that he exists intimidates me. His name is Jordan. I've never spoken to him before.

Their fists are like hammers and each blow hurts. John's eyes, John's words are enough to convince me I deserve this. I am crying like a baby and no part of me is able to fight back. But not even a single one of those blows hurts as much as John's awful words.

Mum cries when she sees me; it's the first thing she does. Later, she loses it big time and threatens blue murder. I tell her it is all my fault. I tell her I picked on a younger boy and his brothers defended him. I ask her not to take the matter further. I tell her we all look as bad as I do. I tell her I gave as good as I got. I beg her not to take the matter further. I tell her I started it.

When the bell goes for break, I pretend that I'm engrossed in my work and even find something to ask the teacher about so I can walk out of the room with her. Even though I don't see Jordan lurking about, I decide to walk with her to the other side of the school. She's quite nice, actually: a bit old, but very approachable. We part at the staffroom and I stroll back towards the garden. An effortless journey, you might think. And so did I, but then I suddenly find myself in the courtyard.

No-Man's-Land.

The girls sitting on the steps next to the door see me before I see them. There are six of them, all seniors, all trying to get their uniforms to look like casual clothes. A girl with curly hair and – I'm a teenager, I'm supposed to notice – rather mature breasts, shouts, "Hey, skinny – what's that ugly thing on your neck? Oh, wait, it's your face!"

They all laugh, and I'd laugh too except I don't find it funny.

"You're so ugly that when you were born…"

"The doctor smacked your mother!" they chorus and then howl with laughter. I try not to notice, to walk faster. I hear them say "weed" as I turn the corner and console myself by thinking that their insults are so corny and old. For some reason, it doesn't help much.

When I tell Thane, he is sympathetic, but amused. "I've spent nights thinking of something suitable to say in reply," he says.

"Nights, I tell you. But nothing seems cruel enough to match their collective spite."

David and Andrea, who met at the party on Saturday, walk past.

"I bet you they're doing it," Thane says.

I decide not to tell him about my encounter with Jordan, who is hopefully taking out his anger on the football pitch. Except we have PE after break and we're playing dodge-ball... I'll hide behind Thane.

"How are things at home?" I ask.

He shrugs.

"They're still at it. I went to Alex's place to play pool all day yesterday. When I got back he had gone into the shed, and she was crying in her room. I haven't spoken to them all weekend."

I ask him who Alex is, and he tells me he's another friend.

English is my favourite subject at this school because Mr Edwards enjoys teaching and is passionate about the subject. He tells us about a poetry competition and invites us all to enter.

"There are no titles," he says, sitting cross-legged on his desk, "but consider this: all of you, at some time, must have paused, in the busy drudgery of adolescence, to wonder what life is all about. And this is healthy and this is natural. Man must at some point – I beg your pardon, all men and women will, at some point, question his or her place in the grand scheme of things. And I'm sure that you must have had, deep in the night, thoughts about where you fit in. When the quiet of the night allows you to query the strange workings of fate."

I wonder how many of us are thinking about the history video? Marmaduke said he wrote poetry when he was at school. Quite a few of us nod.

"So your topic is – share those thoughts with us in your poem – find something to say, even if it is just a puzzling question."

Why did Mum and Dad split up? Why did I have to go and touch John the way I did?

More urgently, the puzzling question is – will Jordan still feel angry with me when we play dodgeball next period? He's not in my English class, which is nice.

He glares at me in the changing rooms. He's not much bigger than I am, but he looks older. I told you, I don't look 15. I look nine. But he leaves me alone, and we all run out to the fields. I should be telling you about how I compare myself to the other boys, but some things are best left private.

Talking about privates…

If I told you that I saw the ball coming towards my crotch at a frightening velocity in slow motion, you would think I was being melodramatic. But this is how it happened. From the corner of my eye, I see Jordan hurl it at me, and I turn in time to see it whizzing through the air, straight for my sensitive spot, in slow motion, I kid you not. And slow is the best way to describe how long it takes for the pain to disappear. And slow is how long it feels when the others laugh while I cry like a baby. It is so bad that I'm sent to the sickroom to lie down, which doesn't help much. The pain is excruciating. I sincerely hope there is no permanent damage. I don't want to break what I haven't yet used (with anyone else but me, that is).

I'm horribly embarrassed that I'm crying so much. I don't care if you don't understand; it is very sore.

The sickroom is sparsely furnished and austerely dull. Nothing here makes you want to stay. When I've calmed down, I hear the voice. Can a voice sound like music? This one does. Can a voice sound like a hug? This one feels like the touch of a mother holding an infant. I cannot make out where it is coming from. It sounds too close to be in the corridor. It could be coming from a room next door. Is there another sickroom next door? Whom do I ask? No. It's coming from outside. A girl is talking to someone.

"Oh, you're looking grand today. Your colour's so pure… and look at you – oh, I've missed you."

I look through the window and see a girl on her knees in the garden. She is wearing rubber gloves and holds garden scissors in her left hand. She is talking to the plants. She looks about 17, but I can't tell with women.

"Now, you know I have to prune these leaves, but you must understand, I do it only because it will help you in the long run. It'll keep you strong and beautiful. Don't look at me like that." She snips and snips. "I'm being as gentle as I can."

You have no idea how beautiful that garden looks. It's like someone's dropped a platter of artists' paints into the soil. The colours almost glow. She has short blonde hair and a long fringe, which she keeps wiping from her eyes. She uses the back of her hand to do this. She's skinny like me.

"And YOU," she says, turning to a plant near the pond, "what am I going to do about you? Every week I pull you out and every week you return. You know what that makes you – don't look away; you can't hide from me. In any other garden, you'd be most welcome, but you attract the insects that eat my prize beauties. So, you tell me. What am I going to do about you? Why don't you stay away? Why do you like this place so much?"

I wish I had the luxury of a split second now, because the words have leapt from my mouth and I've no control.

"He likes it because it's such an incredible place," I say, loud enough for her to hear.

She looks up.

If I said she is the most incredibly beautiful girl that I've ever seen, you would think I'm saying it because my testicles have recently been traumatised, and I've no idea if you'd be right. Her eyes are… dammit, she's lovely.

She is.

"How do you know it's a he?" she asks, smiling.

"All weeds are boys," I reply.

"Are you a weed?"

"Depends in which garden I found myself. I'd probably feel like one in yours, though."

She looks at me for a while and smiles.

"Aaaw, I don't know," she says. "Do you like gardening?"

I shake my head.

"No," I say, "but yours is quite beautiful. The colours are… colourful." Duh.

"So what are you in for?"

"Groin injury," I say.

"Ouch," she says. She could also have said *marzipan* and it would have sounded perfect. She has a brilliant smile.

"How come you're gardening?" I ask.

"It's part of being a senior ecologist. It's my duty to keep the garden looking lovely. It's part of the practical biology course. I love gardening. My little patch of heaven."

"Then that must make you an angel."

She laughs.

"You're such a charmer," she says.

It's not just her voice. She seems really nice. I'm a junior, though. Still...

1. I'm talking without fear to a girl I find ravishing. She reminds me of Auntie Wendy in a way.
2. She's talking back.
3. I do like girls.
4. I now know what I'm going to do my biology project on.

Auntie Wendy is beside herself with joy.

"What's her name?"

"That's just it. I didn't ask."

"The WonderBabe of the Century and you don't ask her name? Have you forgotten all I've taught you?"

"How can I explain? We spoke as if we knew each other for years. It was almost as if there was no need to know each other's names."

How do you explain the fast beating of my heart? I long to see her again. I tried all today, but no show. There is something about this girl that has... no, wait – I mustn't get carried away.

"She sounds wonderful." Auntie Wendy is genuinely pleased. "You never know," she says, "this might be the one for you."

"But she's a senior."

"So?"

"So, seniors don't go for juniors. It's so uncool."

"Don't think for her. You never know."

"Anyway, what about your man?" I ask. "Is love still on the menu?"

I wish I hadn't asked. She tells me in confidence that she heard he was planning to take her overseas. I do not approve.

The balloon...

"Nothing's definite yet," she says. "So no need to worry. You're not getting rid of me that easily."

The pebble feels cold in my hands.

The crowd is standing back. They hush themselves quieter. The sun is setting. The rock pool is like glass. I'm aware that the reporters are reporting but I can't hear what they're saying. Doesn't matter. All that matters is now. I must stay focussed. I hold the pebble up to the judges. Three goes, that's all I have, and all three have to be sixes in order for the record to be recognised. I can feel my heart beat faster. Must stay calm.

The first pebble hops once… twice… twice.

That was a practice round.

"Right, so – here we go then."

Once. Twice. Three times. Four times. Five times… SIX!

The pebble disappears with a plop as the crowd goes berserk.

"Well now the tension's really on. One down, two to go."

Piece of cake. I try to look humble. The pebble just made six hops, but it's good enough. Must stay focussed. I breathe in deeply. I hold up the stone. You can hear a pin drop.

Once… twice… three times…

"And, oh, he's just missed it."

So close.

The trouble with Rhododendrons

Thane is becoming suspicious of my behaviour.

"Where are you dashing off to?" he asks. What he means is: what're you up to? He has that look on his face. I haven't told him about *her* yet.

"I'm in the mood for walking," I say.

"Wait up. I'll walk with you. Where are you going?"

"Exploring," I say. "And I'd rather do it alone."

He looks puzzled, almost hurt. "Ooh. Okay, Mr Garbo."

I'm not quite sure what he means. I know he won't understand. I have to see her. To say that she is the stuff of dreams is an understatement, and hopelessly too polite. It's a magnetic thing. I feel drawn to her. What can I say? I like being around her, that's all.

John catches me looking at him, there. He shakes his head and walks away.

She's neither on the fields nor in the garden where I first saw her. She's not on the hill, and nor is she near the tennis courts. She might be in the biology lab… there's Jordan, quick detour – she's not near the admin block.

You're like a dog chasing a bus, I think. I decide to go back to Thane. He is talking to two people from our class.

"You think you've had a bad day – oh, back are we?" He grins and continues. "Wait until you hear about this. My old man wakes me up because I've overslept and goes ballistic when he sees that my bed is wet. "You're not flipping two years old!" he yells, the veins inflating in his forehead. "Jesus Christ! What is wrong with you?" What is wrong with me is that the bathroom pipes are leaking through my ceiling straight onto my bed, but he doesn't know this. And my old lady, oh, she's a work of art, freaks out and blames my bedwetting on him, and he gets pissed off because she takes my side, and just to prove that she hasn't taken my side, she freaks out at me, and… one of these days, something's going to give in."

"Your ceiling," I say, throwing grass at him.

"My parents never fight," Carl, who hardly says anything, says. "I don't think they know how to."

"Mine are never together long enough to fight," I say, not knowing where that came from. Thane looks up at me and catches my eye. I am uncertain what he is thinking.

"Hey, Deirdre!" Thane calls, and we look up to see her turn around. "Hey, Thane," she answers walking over. "What's happening you old fart?"

"Me Thane," he says, offering to shake her hand. I give him stern looks. "I hear you're having a party soon." She doesn't seem to get the joke.

"Where did you hear that?" She doesn't look convinced.

"Ellie told me," he replies.

"Stupid cow can't – oh, hello, Chris." She smiles at me and turns back to Thane. "Can't keep her fat mouth shut. So? What if I am?"

"We were just wondering, Chris and I, when… when, you know… when we will be receiving our invitations."

"Nathaniel Conrad, after your behaviour at the last party what makes you think I would ever want to invite you to my house again?"

"What's this?" I ask.

"You don't want to know," Thane interrupts.

"Oh, but I do."

"He puked all over my parents' bed," she says, pulling a face. "During a party they did not know I was having. In order to avoid telling them that I had thrown this huge party while they were on holiday, I had to tell them I did it, and they were not impressed. Stop laughing, Thane. You're NOT invited. Chris is. You're not."

"I don't go anywhere without my amigo," I tell her, and Thane's eyes light up.

"Well there's a first for everything," she says, walking away.

I SEE HER!

There she is, at the far end of the corridor. That's definitely her. My heart does a dance as I race between the others to get to her. To get to the Principal, more like it, who reprimands me for running, and by the time I get to where she was, she has disappeared. Typical.

I've been back to her garden, and sure enough, there it is, blowing gently in the wind, the little weed, like some stubborn little thing, back again. This time, I uproot it and take it to my biology teacher. She tells me its name.

"But I thought you wanted to study up on rhododendrons," she says.

For some reason, I'm in a good mood when I get home and even knock on Marmaduke's studio door to say hello. It's open, anyway. I shouldn't have, I know, but I just wanted to say hi, I'm home. I've had a good day.

"Come and look at this," he beckons, showing me the painting he is working on.

It's of a forest at twilight, I think. The more I look, the more animal life I see.

"They want me to produce 12 canvasses representing the bio-diversity of the planet. What do you think?"

"There's so much to see," I say.

"I know, I know, but look." He turns the canvas around and it becomes an underwater scene. He has a look of excitement on his face. I'm overawed.

"All 12 of them are going to be like this," he says. "This is only number three. Maybe you can help me think of a suitable title? Not now, of course. When it's more finished. How was school?"

"I think I'm in love," I say calmly.

Marmaduke grins almost proudly. I really regret not getting her name.

"Well, that calls for a celebration," he says. "Let's go out for milkshakes."

We stop over at an ice-cream café and sit out in the open, waiting for our orders. He questions me about her, but as my knowledge is limited, my answers are by necessity disappointingly brief.

"It's a wonderful feeling, isn't it?" he says cheerfully.

"It's a stupid feeling. I know nothing about her, and she's older than I am. But I think she's terrific."

"Have you had a girlfriend before?" he asks. I decide to tell him.

"I nearly did," I say, "but Auntie Wendy scared her away when she came to visit one Saturday. She brought out all my baby photos. In most of them I don't have any clothes on. And then she started talking about babies and how she would love to be a godmother to my children one day. I think it all put the girl off. She never came to visit again."

"Do you miss her?" he asks. "Auntie Wendy."

I nod. I do.

"It must be hard to lose a sister. Your mother was such a vibrant woman."

"Why did you leave?" I ask.

He shakes his head and sighs.

"It's a long story. I'd rather not go into it now."

"Did you love her very much?" I ask.

"I've always loved her very much. But it is more complicated than that. I remember one time; I think we had been going out for about two years, when I had sold my first painting to an older woman. She was so happy for me, but at the same time, I knew she was jealous. The other woman asked me to visit her often to talk about the paintings she was interested in, and Sarah thought I was being led astray, bless her. So she went to this woman – I don't even remember her name – and had it out with her. Nothing happened. I was never unfaithful. But the determination in your mother's eyes was enough to convince me that she was serious about us. And yet, while I was flattered, it also scared the crap out of me. I will tell you, one day, why I left your mother, but I can't do it now."

I'm in a garden, holding a huge red heart. Not a real heart, of course; a fluffy down-filled one. It is a bright day; the clouds look like cotton wool. I'm two years old. Mum is preparing a picnic. There is so much to eat and just the two of us. I'm on a blanket. I'm wearing a yellow hat.

The sun feels wonderful on my skin. I gurgle and marvel at butterflies flirting in colour. Life is rich and glorious and profoundly magnificent. A butterfly twirls on the breeze and does a loop-the-loop before it lands on the glass flask containing the baby dolphin.

"Whatever you do," Mum had warned me, "don't knock it over."

I reach out to touch the butterfly. Its wings look so delicate, so fragile and pretty, I can't imagine that it could sustain controlled flight. The sun makes me squint and for the shortest of moments, the butterfly's wings catch the rays and seem to explode in colour.

The flask topples. For a split second, it topples in slow motion. I know I have to undo this.

Perhaps if I pull my hand back fast enough, I can reverse the consequences?

The water seeps away; the dolphin flaps pathetically. Then it stops. I try to concentrate my thoughts so that I can somehow tell it telepathically to live again, but this does not work and I cry out loudly.

Mother rushes over in a flurry of anguish. I point to the butterfly, but she knows I did it. She glares at me in disappointment, then angrily packs her things into the car. She rushes over and snatches the big red heart from my hands. I watch her storm off.

I watch her climb into the driver's seat. I watch her drive away.

The sky is so big. The butterflies have gone.

Marmaduke is not here now. My room is filled with shadows, and quiet like the grave. I can hear my heart beating.

Where do you turn when you genuinely don't understand?
Where do you go to bring back the dead?
Who holds you when you come back alone?
What do you do when you don't know what to do?
What can you take for something that cannot heal?
Who do you blame when there's no-one else to blame?

A woman and her son are driving on the motorway. He turns up the volume on the car sound system. She turns it down. "I'll thump you," she says. "I'll thump you," he says, turning the volume louder. She turns it softer. He turns it louder. "Oh, for crying out loud," she says, taking her hands off the steering wheel.

Just for one second.

Close-up of the wheel as the vehicle slides to the left. Close-up on the shard of thick glass. Slow mo: the moment the glass rips into the tyre. Blackout.

I moan myself awake. The room is quiet. I am completely alone.

Thane is cheerful and does a little dance when he sees me. He holds up a library book. "Look what I found," he says, showing me a photograph of a shark attack victim. "Cool or what?"

"You're flipping sick," I say, walking away.

I want things to be the way they were.

I got up at one this morning and wanted to scream at the moon. Instead, I sat at my desk and just started writing. This is my entry for the poetry competition:

The Day Hitler Should Have Died
(or how everything depends on the fraction of a second)

From behind he looks almost frightened, the little boy,
although she cannot see the exhilaration in his eyes,
cannot hear the trumpets of Prussian glories resounding
in his ears.

The other three, bigger, more menacing,
make her think of the bastard asleep upstairs.
Her sharpening the shop's knives
suddenly becomes overwhelmingly significant.

The boy, however, advancing backwards, stops,
and she sees in his defiant stance
the triumph of will over weakness,
the Jacob/Angel story of her life, the struggle.

He launches into what seems to be a diatribe
of mad gestures; insistent and utterly convincing.
She thinks he resembles a crazed minister

making perfect sense.

She thinks: If a boy can stand up to his tormentors,
I can stand up to that cheating bastard asleep upstairs.
That the boy has no need for violence makes her feel guilty.
Her sharpening the knives suddenly becomes significant.

The bullies will wonder for weeks to come how he did it;
how his words, his conviction, could so thoroughly
redirect their anger, their peasant brutality.
They retreated one by one to become soldiers of another war.

Further up the street and out of view, a horse,
fed up and thoroughly pissed off, decides
enough is enough, and, still attached to the cart,
suddenly takes off without his owner
and gallops over the cobbles, determined
not to let anything get in his way.
He has heard far too many stories of stallions slaughtered
on the battlefields, and wants none of it.

It is Austria. It is a long time ago.
Such were the thoughts of horses.
It is a grey clay day. The horse is free
for the first time in its life.
The woman barely has time to think.
She drops the knives – she won't be able to recall
when precisely she knew he was in danger.
The boy stands firm, almost, she thinks,
overestimating his defiance. He thinks the thunderous
clatter roaring down on him is nature, concurring.

She moves in slow motion faster than ever before;
she snatches the boy just in time; she breaks her arm on,
of all things, the grocer's sandwich board, and feels
God smiling on her.

Later she will use the arm and the bruises as evidence
of her husband's brutality, and her brother
will take care of it all one night, and her life will change.
Those few seconds, clasping the child that bastard
made sure she will never have, she felt she belonged,
she knew she had rescued the power to love, and,
her guilt assuaged, her faith restored, she knew
she would never have to sharpen knives again.

By the time she gets to her feet, little Adolf
has run home to his mother. The moment's significance
has passed. Present, past and future collide
when these things happen.

His mother knows nothing of cosmic inevitability,
nothing about the grim irony of fate. She is unable
to share his adventures, unable to comprehend,
oblivious to the noise of regiments marching in his head.

She has no idea how different the world
could have been had the local butcher's wife been deaf;
had a certain horse not been so hungry for change;
had the cat not been sleeping where the knives fell.

by Chris Elliot

I don't know what it means exactly. I did while I was writing it. I don't know where it came from. All I know is it didn't stop coming. Like some flood, the words crashed onto the page. I had to do something to calm my mind, and sleeping was obviously not the way.

I have to confess, though, I did use a thesaurus. I don't usually use words like diatribe. And I also have to add that this was not the first draft. The first draft took two hours. For the rest of the night, I found myself deleting anything that might sound too simple or childlike. I was a bit worried about using "pissed off" because I am not sure if the judges would accept that. I tried replacing it with "angry", but that didn't quite capture it. "aggrieved" sounded too…

I don't know... mild. When I put "pissed off" back in, it sounded just right.

The Jacob/Angel part I borrowed from an RE lesson.

I wanted the poem to sound like it was written by someone far more mature than me... than I. I must have re-read and redrafted the thing for hours, because when I looked up, the sun had already risen. It still doesn't sound right. It is still not exactly what I want to say.

I must not get angry about this. I have read it and re-read it so often that now even I don't know what it means any more. I don't care if it doesn't win; at least I have the guts to submit the thing. Let others try and work it out. I think I wrote it out of anger. The only reason I am going to school today is to hand the damn thing in.

I went for a walk just before school, but that did not help. I'm in such a bad mood. I just want the world to go away. I just want to stay home and, no, not sleep, hide. I didn't mean to snap at Thane. I know he has it tough at home, but at least his mother is still alive. I would do anything to have my mother back.

If only I really believed in God, I could bargain with him for her return.

Bad moods are like an infectious disease. I tell myself not to feel so glum, but instantly tell myself to shut up. It is like there is this other me, and he's a real evil little shit. Every time I want to get angry at God, or even Mum for leaving me, I end up back at the same place: hating myself.

I can't stand school. I hate being by the sea. Auntie Wendy could have done something. As my teachers drone on and on, I find a sea of resentment rising within me. I don't care if they are trying to educate me. I don't care if the sum of the hypotenuse equals the square of a mosquito's backside. I don't want to be here.

Here.

I looked at myself in the mirror this morning and saw nothing I liked. I look ugly when I cry. I want to burst, but I look ugly when I cry.

Something inside keeps telling me to fight this, despite myself.

Let Jordan try to take me on. In fact, I want him to take me on. I want him to…

Let go, let go.

And when the opportunity presents itself, I seize it hungrily. We are in the art class, trying to sculpt trees. I need to get more clay and have to pass his chair on the way. He is engrossed in his work. I accidentally bump his chair with my foot and his carving knife slips, damaging his efforts. He immediately gets up, and I'm ready for him.

"Sorry," I say insincerely.

"That's taken me hours," he says, and it takes me a few seconds to realise that he is not angry. "Shit, man." He shakes his head, and if I didn't know better, looks as if he is going to cry. Instead, he mumbles some obscenity and sits down again.

Typical.

Thane ruffles my hair.

"Piss off," I tell him.

"Hey, hey, hey," he catches up with me. "What's this? Where's Chris and what have you done with him?"

"Leave me alone," I say, crossing the road to get to the beach. "Go away."

Thane looks at me in utter amazement.

"What's up with you?"

I decide not to answer him.

"Is something happening at home?" Even though I walk fast, he keeps up with me. "Is it your dad? Is it your mum?"

"Will you stop flipping asking me about my mother, alright?!"

The force with which this is said stuns even me. I will never forget the look on Thane's face.

Like I had just shot him. *Or kissed him.*

"Okay," he backs off. "Whatever." He shakes his head and walks away. "You know, a problem shared is a problem solved," he calls in Mrs Flank's voice.

I don't reply.

I make my way to the rock pool but now suddenly don't feel like being there.

PEBBLE CHAMPIONSHIP POSTPONED

When I get home, I remind myself not to snap at Marmaduke. He's in his studio though, so the risk is reduced. I go straight to my room, draw the curtains, curl up into a little ball and try to disappear.

When my father asks what I would like for dinner, I tell him that I'm not hungry.

When he wakes me up the next morning, I tell him I'm not feeling well.

When he asks if I would like to see a doctor, I tell him to leave me alone.

The waves are loud today. I want them to be louder. There's a strong breeze. I can't go to my rock pool for fear of being seen by anyone from school, so I head in the opposite direction.

How do I let go, Mum?

How do I let go when I know that it would mean I've forgiven myself, and I can't?

I decide to call Auntie Wendy from a call box next to the beach café, and despite myself, find myself crying on the phone.

"Oh, my baby," she says, "I know it hurts. I know how sore it is. But we have to soldier on, and with time, we are able to. Give it time, Chris."

To my shame, I cannot tell her the real reason. I tell her I want to see her. I need to see her.

She suddenly goes very quiet.

"Auntie Wendy?"

"I've got bad news, Chrissie."

More silence.

"I'm… I'm leaving tomorrow morning," she says.

Our little yellow Fiat skids along the road.

"I was going to call you this evening," she says.

Our little yellow Fiat crashes into a pole.

"Christopher?"

Hours later, I see Deirdre rounding the corner. I'm on my way home. I smile when I see who is with her.

"Hey, Chris," she says. "Where were you today?"

"You're the boy with the groin injury," the other girl says.

Typical. We meet on one of my bad days. I must not let them see.

"I had a dodgy tummy," I say, and then, with as much confidence as possible, but cool enough to be casual, I turn to the other girl and say, "You're the girl with the weed problem. How does your garden grow?" I kid you not.

She looks genuinely happy to see me.

"You know each other?" Deirdre asks.

"We met in my garden. Well, you weren't in the garden, you were in the…"

"Sickroom," we both say together.

"Are you coming to the party?" she asks. "We'll both like it if you do."

I don't care.

"I'll bring flowers," I say without hesitation.

"Oh, no, don't," she says. "I much prefer them in the ground. They live longer that way."

When they walk away, despite Auntie Wendy's dreadful news, and despite my foul mood, I find myself smiling.

She likes me.

The clouds are clearing.

The dolphin is pleased to see me. It lets me hold its fin. We glide through the water and I'm laughing. I know I'm not allowed to, but I don't care.

The sun sets slowly. The beach is full. My rock pool beckons.

Part Two
Holding On

Must be a puberty thing

As soon as I kiss him, John pushes me away, and stands up. He is shaking his head, and I am shaking.

The words "I'm sorry" crouch at the back of my throat, too scared to come out. John looks bewildered, and a bit frightened.

"I am not like that," he announces finally. "And if you ever touch me there again, I'll punch you. I'm not like that."

This from my best friend.

"Neither am I. I was joking," I reply. "Honest."

John moves to walk away. Our wrestling game is over.

"No you weren't," he says.

Please don't tell anyone, I scream in my head every time I see him.

So why did he?

Her name's Evelyn. God was good the next day. I see her and Deirdre again, at school, during break, sitting on the football stands, watching some boys play rugby. Well, I say I see them. What I actually mean is, I followed Deirdre out onto the fields in the hope that I'd see them.

She is truly the most remarkable girl I've ever met. And, I'm probably exaggerating and being clichéd, but I'm a teenager, I'm besotted, and that's all there is to it.

No, you're not. You're just…

Shut up, Chris.

She smiles like the sun, and, more importantly, she beams at me. "Hello, Christopher."

I want to dissolve into marshmallowy gooeyness, and all I can think of is two words: *be nice.* Mum might have thought love had spots, but I'm not letting Evelyn near the icky parts of my personality. Be nice. Be the kind of guy that she can't help but like.

"You've got jam on the side of your mouth," I say.

Parts of me want to kiss it clean, but I would never dream of doing that. Not in front of Deirdre, anyway. I'd offer the tissue in my pocket, but I sneezed into it earlier so that's out of the question.

"Thanks," she says, using her handkerchief to wipe it away. "Not just any jam," she says, holding the smear for me to admire. "Homemade with home-grown berries. Yummy."

"So where's your amigo?" Deirdre asks. I shrug. He's avoided me all morning. Can't say I blame him. Don't care now. Will worry about that later.

"How's your groin?" Evelyn asks. She lifts the bag next to her and says, "Sit down. You hungry?" I shake my head.

"My groin's fine," I reply.

"Bet it is," Deirdre says.

I try to give her an Auntie Wendy look. Not my favourite person at the moment, Auntie Wendy. I suddenly realise that she should be on her flight right now. I look up at the sky, half expecting to see a plane.

"Such sad eyes," Evelyn says to Deirdre. "Don't you think? Sad eyes."

"And what would I have to be sad about?" I ask.

"I don't know," Evelyn smiles. "You tell me."

"Maybe he's missing someone back in London?" Deirdre says, raising her eyebrows.

"Oh, yes. Deirdre said you were new here. So do you?" Evelyn asks.

I've heard the expression silky soft skin in adverts and books, but hers is super, double deluxe, luxury super-perfect soft, or at least, it looks it.

"Do I what?"

"Do you miss someone in London?"

"No," I say quickly, because it's true and I don't feel like playing games.

Auntie Wendy called last night, but I asked Marmaduke to tell her that I was sleeping and not feeling well, which was mostly true. I know she told me she was in love, and that now I was here, she wanted to live her life to the full. I know I should understand and be really happy that she's happy, but I feel betrayed and abandoned. Not here, right now with Evelyn, but last night, when the shadows came alive, and the floodgates buckled, and the balloon inside me pressed hard against my heart. Last night was the second worst night of my life.

John's mother is at the door. Suddenly, I believe in God and pray fervently that John hasn't said anything. I strain to hear what she is saying, and my worst fears come true. The only place to hide is under the bed, and I am not going to do that.
"Is it true?" Mum asks, when John's mother leaves.

Does she like me? She's very friendly. I haven't said anything stupid, yet. I don't want her or Deirdre to know how I feel. Playing it cool requires some sort of swagger, and I do not have one that is convincing enough. So I'll just play it me, shiny side up.
"So you're coming to the party?" Evelyn asks.
"Only if you'll be there."
"What a charmer. Of course I'll be there. You can meet my boyfriend, James."
At the fishery, a dolphin is slit open down the middle and its insides topple out onto a wooden deck.

I'm not angry. I'm not in a bad mood. I do not feel like shouting or raging at the heavens. As the bell rings and I make my way back to class, I know exactly what I feel like: a hug.
Of course she has a boyfriend. She's a senior and she's beautiful. I'm 15, and lately something of a cry-baby. But I won't cry now. No balloons press against my insides. It just feels hollow.
And besides, who was I trying to fool?
Mum is hugging me. She tells me that puberty can be confusing, and that is all part of growing up.
"You'll meet a nice girl, you'll see."

Thane is leaning against the wall next to the school gates. I have to walk past him to go home. Is he angry with me for being so moody?

"Hey you," he says, as I approach.

"Hey yourself."

"Ooh."

"Ooh yourself," I reply.

"Aha," he says.

"Aha yourself."

"Be…"

"I would if I know who that was."

He grins.

"You too? Must be a puberty thing. I'm thinking of going for a swim," he says. A mischievous looks makes itself at home on his face. "At your place. Coming?"

Later, he asks, as we drape our towels over the railings and sit with our feet in the water, "So what's been eating you lately?"

"It's a long story."

"Good."

"But I don't want to go into it. How're things at home?"

"Don't ask."

"Just did, twitface."

"It's a long story."

"When has that ever stopped you?"

I slide into the water and swim to the other side. He drops in and sits cross-legged underwater. He is pretending to meditate. I dive under and try to walk like an Egyptian.

Later, we lie down on the warm paving surrounding the pool, and I say, "I'm sorry about yesterday. I shouldn't have taken it out on you."

"You had me worried." He rolls over onto his tummy. "You sounded like my parents."

"It's my aunt. She left the country this morning to follow a complete stranger overseas. Just like that. I won't see her again for a very long time."

"So you decided to take it out on your best friend?" Thane shakes his head in mock disbelief.

"So you're my best friend now, are you?"

"Well you don't have any other friends here, so I'll have to do."

"Yet. I don't have any other friends, yet."

"Whatever. I think it's quite romantic, your aunt falling in love and deciding to leave. It's very impulsive. I'd do the same if some girl asked me to go with her, which is about as likely as my folks learning to get along. Anyway, you should be happy for her."

Some girl.

"That's what I keep telling myself," I say. "But it doesn't make it easier to accept."

"Life's about learning to let go. Would you rather she was miserable and alone?"

"No," I say. "That is the last thing I would ever want. Ever."

"So let her go. If that makes her happy, let her go. She wouldn't want you to be unhappy and lonely." He sits up.

"By leaving, she's made me that way," I say.

"You're unhappy because she's in love."

"No."

"Then don't worry about it then. Life's too short. But talking about love, I happened to see you spending break with Deirdre today. Anything you're not telling me? The grapevine's buzzing like a beehive."

"I was talking to her friend about my biology project." I shake my head. "What grapevine's this?"

"Well, according to Ellie, who is our very own beloved and nurtured walking broadcasting corporation, Deirdre's been telling people that she thinks you're *charming* and *shy*. Apparently, she's holding this party in the hope that you will be there."

"Bullshit," I say.

"Mmm," he replies. "More than likely, I made the last bit up. Silly me. But not the bit about her liking you. And now, she thinks, because you spent break with her, that you want to ask her out, but you're too shy. It's so romantic. Apparently, she thinks you're going to do it at the party."

"Do what?" There should be multiple question marks here.

"Ask her out," he says, and grins when he sees me sigh. "I don't think she puts out yet, but you never know with religious types."

"She's religious?"

"No, but her father is. He's a minister of the church. So are you going to?"

"Don't people have anything better to do than gossip about strangers?"

"You're not a stranger, Chris. You're part of our warm little family now. Everybody knows everybody's business. This is how it is on The Rock, which is what we call the island, by the way."

"Sounds like Alcatraz," I say. "That's a bit bizarre. People I don't know speculating about my life."

"That's life. So are you?"

"You sound like a spy," I say.

"Maybe I am? Are you?"

"Am I a spy?"

"You're going in the pool now. You don't know it yet," he advances, like Frankenstein's monster with his arms lifted, "but soon you will find yourself thrown into the murky depths."

Agent Chris Elliot has a split second to decide what to do.

Marmaduke opens his studio door when he hears me come in. His smile is generous and friendly

"How are you doing, son? You look better."

Son.

"I'm sorry about yesterday," I say. "Not a good day for me."

"I spoke to Auntie Wendy last night. She says you were quite abrupt on the phone."

I'm not sure whether he is telling me off.

"It was a bit of a shock. It was just so sudden."

"I know," he says gently. "This came for you."

He hands over a postcard from London. It's of Big Ben. It's from Auntie Wendy. I smile first because she and I share a private joke about Big Ben. Then I read what she wrote: *I'm in love. Please forgive me. Try to understand. I will never stop loving you.*

"Do you think I'm being melodramatic when I say I feel I'm losing everyone I ever cared for?" I look up as I ask this. "Am I being a baby for letting this hurt me? I'm trying to be strong, but I don't know how."

"I tell you what," he suggests, "let's get something to drink and we can talk on the balcony."

You see what I mean? Weird thoughts. I walk through the door and pour my heart out without thinking. Marmaduke tells me not to worry and adds that everything I'm going through is natural.

"Kris," he says. "I'm worried about your nightmares. You don't talk much about your feelings. I think you should start talking about your dreams. I take back what I said about not disturbing me while I'm busy. I just feel we should talk about these nightmares. I think it'll help."

"I don't remember them most of the time," I lie. "They're all about Mum."

Not strictly speaking true.

"It's going to take time," he says.

The view from our balcony is nothing short of magnificent.

"I know," I say. "Everything takes time. That's what everyone says. Give it time. Everyone's telling me that. But it doesn't help now."

"If you ever feel like you did yesterday, don't even bother knocking, just come and chat. I know there's nothing that can take away the pain, but locking yourself in your room won't make it easier. To be honest, I felt... I feel... sometimes, especially yesterday... hopeless, or rather, helpless... when it comes to making the pain go away. It really will help to talk."

"Why do we have to let go of the people we love?" I ask.

"Because that's how we prove we love them."

It's not a satisfactory answer, but as he speaks, I see in his eyes a man who is serious about me. Some stubborn thing inside me tells me not to criticise what he is saying but, like observing his paintings, to look for the reasons behind the words.

I've been very selfish lately. He misses her too, and how awful for Auntie Wendy to lose a sister she's known for 36 years. They too have to let go of Mum, but how is it they manage to let go without falling, without falling apart?

"The memories sustain us," he explains. "It's also easier if you think of your Mum like Auntie Wendy: Wendy's gone, but she's going someplace. Sarah's gone, but she's someplace too. I must confess that I know I'm losing myself in my work in an effort to shield the pain. I'm sorry if you felt you couldn't speak to me yesterday. I feel I should be giving you advice on how to cope with all of this," he says. "All I can say is, if you want time to heal, just keep going. It will get easier. I promise."

Marmaduke has brown eyes, soft brown eyes.

He tells me the nice thing about life is that it weeds out all bad memories and allows only the good to remain. I've got to find the courage to keep going because that's what we all have to do – that's what life demands of us. He says that when things get rough for him, he thinks of the times he had with Mum. They shared many incredible moments, and knowing he had shared those times with her helps him realise that life is good, is full of wonderful moments. He recounts the time they went on holiday, camping in the mountains.

"We hadn't started going out then. A bunch of us decided to rough it for the weekend and get away from the final end of year exams. We were in the first year of university. I was madly in love with her, but she wanted us to be friends only. Admittedly, we were best friends, but I was determined. I knew she hated soppy behaviour, so when we were together, I behaved like a friend. Yet, I always made sure that when we were apart, she'd find some little token of my affection lying around. We were all huddled around a small and inefficient fire. As it turned out, the others in the party ended up in pairs: Andrew and Graham, Steve and Jenny, which left Sarah and me. It was the first time we ever slept in the same place together: a tent near a river. Alone. She looked at me, and I looked at her, and we looked at the others looking at each other. I wondered if she was aware of the dynamics emerging as the evening wore on. At some point, we would all have to say goodnight and go to our respective tents. I wondered if she was thinking what I was thinking. She didn't appear uncomfortable. Or nervous. Or in any way romantically persuaded by the surroundings. I left a flower on her sleeping bag. Do you know what she said when she saw it?" He looks at me enquiringly and I shrug. "'Why did you kill it? It was much happier growing wherever you found it. Thanks anyway, though.'

And she pecked me on the cheek like she always did. 'Tomorrow,' she said, 'you will walk me to the spot and we can admire it together.' And she climbed into her sleeping bag and I climbed into mine and she spoke about the exams and I wanted to tell her how I felt, but I knew she already knew, and I knew how she felt. Friends only. I was really hoping something would happen that night. I was 19 – who can blame me? I knew if anything was to happen it would be initiated by her, and that if I made any kind of move whatsoever, it would end in a fight. But what did happen, though, was the next day, when we went for a walk alone together, she made us climb a tree. And sitting on a branch, she said, 'To me, you are like this tree: a strong, dependable friend who provides shelter from the storm. I know how you feel for me, M. –' that was what she called me, 'and I'm flattered. But if anything was to happen between us, and if I fell for you in that way, there would only be one inevitable conclusion. Like the tree, you will always be reaching for the sun – you're going to be a successful artist one day, I truly believe that, but I want someone who is reaching just for me.'"

Marmaduke looks up at the moon.

"The way she said it, the tone of finality, made me want her even more, even though she was breaking my heart. My head was saying, I know that, but my heart was saying, I want to be yours. I didn't give up, though. Just as she was determined that we should become friends, I was determined to make her fall in love with me."

"How long did it take?" I ask. I realise I'm still holding the postcard.

"About two years," he says. "That long. It was worth it, though."

Two years. Will it be that long before Evelyn breaks up with her boyfriend? Given the nature of most teenage relationships, maybe not. But then again – she is quite lovely – she looks the type who takes relationships seriously. Who am I trying to kid? She won't go for me. She likes me just as a friend. Well, we haven't actually got round to the friendship part either. Maybe that is all I should hope for?

I know what you are doing.

Listen to me. I should be listening to Marmaduke. He's right: I must start remembering only the good things.

But remembering inflates the balloon.

Being here is good, listening to him talk about Mum. The more he speaks, the more I understand that she had a whole life before she had me. What happened to all her dreams?

"Listen to this," I say, picking up the postcard. I read it to him. His expression changes. It's as if the words have unlocked something. It looks as if he is flinching. I want to talk about Auntie Wendy.

"Can I have a look at that?" he asks, and I show it to him. His expression becomes very serious. He goes quiet.

"What's wrong?" I ask softly.

He tries a smile and fails.

"Those were the exact words Sarah used when I left."

How could Auntie Wendy just leave me like that? No, no, no. She's happy now; she's in love. I must try to look on the bright side. I try to imagine her face, smiling, in the arms of someone who can finally take good care of her. Would I rather she was miserable and back in the city? A part of me does. But I won't let it corrode the other part. I do want Auntie Wendy to be deliriously happy. I'm just a) jealous that it is not me who makes her smile, b) jealous that she's in love, c) lonely now that she's gone. Lonely not only because I will miss our chats on the phone and her company but also because she is the closest link I have to Mum.

As I listened to Marmaduke earlier, I became aware of just how much I like him. He takes life so calmly, so quietly. It's hard to believe that although he seems soft-spoken on the outside, his paintings reveal an active, vibrant and very original mind. It's easy for me to admire him. But why couldn't he and Mum get along? I want to be like him. I want to be creative. What, though, am I good at? I can't paint like he can. I can't act like Thane can. I'm no good at sports, although I like swimming. How much of his good looks have I inherited? I'm no good at gardening. I like poetry. I wrote some before Mum died. I can't believe I actually handed in that poem. I cannot believe I actually wrote it. Where did it come from? Why did it all just come out? Where did the desire to keep changing it come from? Normally, I don't like redrafting things. Normally, it takes me time to write anything. That poem just poured out and then demanded to be corrected and amended, as if I was writing what someone else was telling me to write. Weird. Like these dreams. I'm not usually one for remembering my dreams, but these are so vivid that they are almost overbearing. Perhaps I need to understand them better? Perhaps, as Marmaduke says, I need to analyse them carefully? I mean, many ancient cultures regarded dreams as messages, although Miss Alwyn said that they were just the mind doing housekeeping chores, whatever that means. Our RE teacher said that dreams are the window to the subconscious. If that's the case, I'd rather keep my blinds drawn. I am having a hard enough time facing reality; I don't think I have the energy to tackle my nightmares.

On the beach later, I collect pebbles for a stint at the rock pool.

"It's an incredible evening," the first commentator says. "A very substantial crowd has already gathered in preparation for this evening's Championship Challenge.

"And believe me, this is no ordinary challenge: Dodge Johnson has already scored two sixes in the trials. I know he's confident, I know he's itching to claim the title for himself instead of sharing it with someone else."

"Right – and I bet Chris Elliot wants the same thing. Chris scored only one six in the trials. I think he knows he's got a tough evening ahead."

"And what a beautiful evening it is too, Michael: the sun is setting, the sky is warm and orange. The surface, by the way, is glass smooth. One could not hope for a more remarkable setting. Chris Elliot takes his place. He'll be going second. James "Dodge" Johnson is about ready to start."

It's the name. When I look at him, I feel nothing. I know that everyone is counting on me. I can see Evelyn among the crowd. I don't like him because he's the favourite to win tonight. He looks smugly at me as if to say, she's mine.

"So who's your money on, Mike?"

"Funny you should say that because, although Johnson has had more experience, Elliot is not one to back down too easily. It'll be experience versus guts and good luck."

"You haven't answered my question."

"My money's on Johnson, Dave. He knows how to handle the pressure of such a challenge. Elliot's good, but I don't think he has it in him just yet."

Johnson steps forward and holds up his pebble. The crowds become still. He bends his knees slightly and twists his body as he hurls the pebble. It bounces once... twice... three times... four times...

"Oh, this is looking good."

... Five times... SIX!

The applause is deafening. I must stay focussed. I must have faith in myself. I must remind myself that I can cope with anything. I step forward, hold up the pebble. I wait for the crowds to quieten. I can see Evelyn. I can see something in her eyes willing me on. I have to do it.

One... two... three... four – imagine this in slow motion – Five... SIX!

"Oh my, the relief on his face is clearly evident. What a moment."

Evelyn looks so happy; like she's going to burst. She is jumping up and down with the rest of them. People are chanting my name. The sun is so yellow.

Johnson steps forward. He looks up at the sky as if to say a little prayer.

His pebble hops six times. He raises his fists to the sky. I try not to look at Evelyn. Behind her, I see Thane. He has taken his shirt off and is waving it at me. I try not to look at his chest.

"Well, I tell you – I wouldn't want to be in Chris Elliot's shoes right now for all the world. The pressure he is under."

"Mind you, he looks very composed. He holds up his pebble. Look at that for steely concentration. He prepares himself and..."

I thought it just made seven hops, but the judges declared it a six.

There is a slight breeze that lifts James' hair as he stares at the pool and the pebble. Evelyn looks very anxious – don't look there – he throws. The surge of joy that rushes through me as I watch his pebble sink after four nearly knocks me over. All too soon it is my turn. I must not buckle. I can do this. I must believe in myself. Jesus, my hands are sweating. What if it slides out wrong and does a dive? Don't think that. Stay focussed. I wipe my hands. I reach for my pebble.

CHRIS ELLIOT'S DAY OF GLORY.

The reporters shove microphones at me.

"Mr Elliot, how does it feel to have reached your goal?"

"This is not my goal. I want to achieve seven hops."

"But you must be pleased you demolished Dodge Johnson?"

I smile wryly.

A soft mist has rolled in. Evelyn sits on the sand with her arms around her legs, trying to peer at the sea. She has just broken up with her boyfriend and looks sad. She sees a figure near the rocks. She smiles when she realises who it is. She can't help but compare Christopher to James. It has taken her a while, but she sees in Chris all the qualities she is looking for.

Behind her, Thane beckons.

That's only the first part of my dream. The rest of it is more lurid and implausible.

When I see Thane the next day, he is wearing sunglasses. I can still see the bruises under his eye. He tells me he walked into a wall.

"No way. I'm your best friend, you can't fool me." I lift the glasses and wince. His right eye is swollen and bruised purple. "Oh, dear God."

"It's the new look. I took on my father and lost," Thane says. "Won't do that again in a hurry."

Again, I want to hug him. Just for comfort, you understand. But I don't.

"Does it hurt?" Stupid question.

I cannot believe a parent can hit a child. The whole notion is so utterly unfamiliar. Mum never hit me, not even a spanking. She'd explode, and you were sure there would be no survivors, but afterwards she'd apologise for her outburst and ask me what lesson I had learned from the experience. She had a thing about getting me to understand why I had upset her, making me think about how I could avoid such an outburst again.

"I'm so sorry," is all I can say to Thane.

"I cannot wait," he says, "'til I'm old enough to move out. Do you know what this is about?" He points to the eye. "I was arguing with the old lady about something and I called her something I shouldn't have. The old man barges in all guns blazing and demands that I apologise. I say no and his fists do the rest of the talking. Jesus, what a hypocrite. I picked up the words from him."

I thought I had it bad.

"And I know what'll happen when I get home. He'll be pissed on the sofa watching inane chat show programmes and blurting obscenities at the world. He was made redundant recently. And he'll feel all guilty and ask me sit beside him so that he can give me his puppy dog look and rub his knuckles in my scalp, and my mother will shout, 'Leave him alone. Don't you think you've caused enough damage for one day?' And he'll call her a stupid bitch and giggle as if I was in on it." Then he says, "I envy your life. It's peaceful. Watch out – Deirdre alert."

She has spotted us and comes running over. I'm hoping to see Evelyn with her, but she's on her own, and by the looks of things, quite pleased to see me.

"Hi, Chris!" she says to me. To Thane, she says, "Hello you. It's an improvement." To me, she says, looking into my eyes with a broad smile, "You'll never guess."

"Guess what?" I reply.

"You used to be a primate in your previous existence?" Thane ventures.

"Well at least I have evolved," she retorts, and to me, says, "Come on, guess." She looks at me as if I should know the answer.

"I don't know."

"Go on, guess."

"Rumplestiltskin," Thane interrupts. "Oh, no, I've got it. You've decided to come out and confess that you're a lesbian?"

"Go screw yourself," she says.

"At least it's with someone I know and love," he replies.

"Chris," she says, "can't you guess?"

I shrug and admit defeat.

"I've decided Thane can come along to my party too, but only if it's with you."

"That's it?" I ask. "That's what I'm supposed to guess?"

She nods.

"How noble," Thane interjects sarcastically. "By the way, you're drooling."

Deirdre stares at him and he grins back. "The only reason," he says, "that you've changed your mind, is because you want to nab Chris here. It's so obvious, Deirdre."

"Whatever," she replies. "Anyway, see ya."

I look at Thane and Thane looks at me.

"She's after your blood, no doubt about it."

Our smiles spread simultaneously. But we are gentlemen. We wait until she is out of earshot before laughing out loud.

Mr Edwards asks to speak to me after class. He tells me he is very impressed with my poem. He asks if it is original, but I'm not insulted. I tell him how I couldn't sleep, how it just came to me.

"It's a remarkable piece of writing," he says. "I wonder if you'd care to indulge me – I'm keen on giving you a senior exam paper to try. It's an essay exam. The topics are quite challenging. I'm keen to see how you respond to it. Would you mind? It's not compulsory or for marks or anything."

I shrug.

"Sure, why not?"

"Good. Well, stay after school on Friday then. In my room."

I don't see Evelyn at all. I thought it best to hang out with Thane during break time. He looked as if he could do with a friend. Just before the day ends, I sneak into Evelyn's garden to hide a few shells I picked up on the beach on my way home last night. I'll let her try to work out who they're from.

Some stubborn thing won't let go; something stubborn won't hold on.

The boy from the bus… whatshisname… Darryl, is at my house. I do not know how he got here, but he wants me to teach him how to swim. We talk as if we have known each other for years. He tells me he has been walking up and down the beach hoping to bump into me. He tells me he knows how I feel, and he tells me he doesn't mind. He tells me that it is natural. He tells me this while we swim naked underwater.

I wake, not crying, not moaning. The night is still. I listen to the sound of the sea. I am trying not to feel guilty. I need to take a shower. Tomorrow I am going to make Evelyn fall in love with me.

Party animal

I've decided to surprise Thane: I'm going to his house to wake him up and drag him to the beach. I've made a flask of hot coffee. It's five in the morning. Don't ask me why I'm waking up so early. I was up late last night working on my biology project. I had no idea plants were so interesting. This does not mean that I need to get a life, it's simply the more I read up on them, the more I find them fascinating.

For instance, when a volcano erupts and creates a new island, the first life form that appears is the plant, in some form or other. Mankind covering the world with concrete does not deter the green shoots from somehow finding a way through the cracks. Incredibly resistant. Rain or shine, wind or flood, the humble plant survives it all. Even Evelyn-proof. Like some stubborn thing, it won't go away. It bravely asserts its right to be here, to reach for the sun despite avid gardeners like Evelyn determined to weed it out.

Thane's house is about ten minutes from mine, sandwiched between a general store and a service station. The paint on the outside walls has begun to peel in places. The streets are quiet. I know better than to knock on the front door. Thane's window is down the side of the house. The gate squeaks loudly, and a dog starts barking somewhere.

Agent Chris Elliot checks his watch. Ominous music begins. There's not much time left. He wishes he had brought a flask of coffee instead of this mortar missile.

I find Thane's window and knock softly, which is silly really, because the object is to wake him up. I knock a bit harder, afraid that

I might wake his parents. It is not Thane's face I see at the window. I've got it wrong.

"Who the hell are you?" Thane's father asks curtly. His hair looks as if it is trying to escape his head in panic. He is unshaven and not amused. I'm convinced if he had a gun he'd shoot me. The morning face of a drunkard. I'm scared shitless. I stammer an apology and attempt to explain that I'm looking for Thane.

"It's six o'bloody clock in the morning! Jesus Christ!" I hear another voice behind him and wonder if it is too late to make a run for it. I'm so scared I want to cry.

"It's someone for Nathan – bloody six o'clock in the morning." He turns to me again. "Go on, get lost! Bloody kids!"

I don't need a second invitation. As I close the gate, I hear him shout Thane's name. Oh, shit. I'm cringing at the thought of the trouble I've caused my friend.

Shit, shit, shit.

I look back once at the house before turning the corner and making my way to the beach, or, more likely, home. Oh, dear. Oh, damn. If this is what it is like for Thane all the time, how does he cope? How does he manage to be so cheerful, so playful? I've been so self-obsessed. My problems are nothing compared to his.

"Chris!"

I turn to see Thane running towards me. He is wearing tracksuit bottoms and my jumper.

"I'm so sorry, Thane. Shit, I'm so sorry."

He shakes his head and holds up both hands. "Chris, meet my old man; oldcraphead, meet Chris. Don't do that again, please. Are you okay? What is it you wanted?"

"I thought we'd get back to the simple things in life." I hold up the flask. He smiles.

"You crazy twit," he says.

"Is he like that all the time?" I ask, as we make our way to the beach.

"Most of the time. Charming man. Avoid if at all possible."

Today's a bank holiday. I've done my homework. We have the rest of the morning and the whole day ahead. Although the coffee warms us up a bit, hunger soon drives us to my place and breakfast.

Thane mentions how he met Marmaduke the morning he came to fetch me, and how cool he is.

"Like I said, I envy your life." He doesn't mention my mum, which is a relief. He mentions his, though.

"She's just as bad as the old man," he says. "Permanently pissed off. She was a beauty queen, you know. Seriously. But she's not that pretty now. She was going to follow a career in modelling. I think she would have been quite successful. Then she met my old man and they had me… I guess she's pissed off with us for ruining her life. I don't know why they don't just get a divorce."

I wonder again what dreams Mum had. Surely it did not entail being a single parent? I do not remember ever hearing Marmaduke and her fighting. Or do I?

After breakfast, Thane and I take a hike along Shanklin beach around Knock Cliff and Horse Ledge, which, he tells me, is only accessible at low tide. We reach the spot I had found the other day, but travel further, over the boulders and slippery rocks, avoiding the rough spray. Although the weather looked promising, it is now becoming overcast.

"You don't want to get stuck here when the tide comes in," he says. "The water comes right up to the base of the cliffs." We have said little on our journey so far, but suddenly Thane stops, sits down and says, "Have you ever thought about dying?" I check his expression to see where this is going. He looks serious.

"I don't like thinking about death," I reply. "Why worry about it 'til it happens? Why do you ask?"

He shrugs.

"I've been thinking a lot about it lately. Not dying – death. The state of non-being. Not being alive. Is it eternal sleep, or just a short nap before assuming some other form? I wonder what happens after? If it is eternal sleep, then what's the point? I've been studying up on sharks. It's amazing how quickly they close in on their prey. One silent whoosh, slicing through the water, and then the teeth tears at your flesh and you are fish-food. Just like that."

"Maybe that is all we are – food for other things? All life is food for other life."

"Not when you're at the top of the chain. Surely we have some higher purpose? Oh, God – what a frightening thought: maybe we exist purely to add nutrients to the soil when we die, and no other function, no other reason for being here?"

"There must be a reason."

"Yes, but what if that's it? That's the reason. That's all there is to it?"

"What about cremation?" Mum was cremated. "Doesn't that upset your theory a bit?"

"Not at all," he says. "It confirms that we've lost our purpose in life. Now all we do is pass the time, hoping for things to get better."

"Why so deep so early in the day?" I ask. Thane looks at me for a while. Our eyes lock. His mouth shows traces of a smile.

"You're right," he says. "It's a holiday, I'm nowhere near my parents, I'm with a good friend and I'm not in trouble. Time to be frivolous. Let's do drugs."

"But we don't have any drugs."

"Okay, then. Let's build sandcastles."

And we do. Thane builds his close to the water's edge, and I warn him about the incoming tide.

"That's the whole point," he tells me. "Sandcastles are not meant to last."

A bit later I ask, having wanted to ask this for a long time, "Thane? How come you're friends with me?"

He turns his head slightly as if waiting for me to go on. I'm half-afraid he is going to say something flippant.

"Because you're you and you don't pretend to be anyone else," he says. "And because you don't interrupt my silences."

The water rushes up behind him and stretches its way to the rim of the moat. A poorly constructed turret crumbles.

"And because nobody else wants to be friends with me," he adds, laughing.

We throw stones at rusty Coke cans, and I find a few gems to use at the rock pool tonight. We also feed the seagulls bits of our bread, before searching the rocks for washed-up treasures. We cartwheel on the sand and chase each other to the water. Just after noon, we head back to my place for lunch.

It is official: I've got the coolest father in the world. He likes Thane and invites us to play pool with him in a pub round the corner. When there are three of us, Thane comes alive, cracking jokes and making witty remarks. If you look at him, as I do today, you'd think he didn't have a care in the world. I'd like to be Thane, but I wouldn't like to be in his shoes. I like seeing Thane and Marmaduke laughing together.

We're not just passing the time.

"There's something about Thane's eyes," Marmaduke says, later that evening, when we are alone at home. But he doesn't go on to qualify the statement.

The courtroom is stuffy and quiet like a church. The prosecutor steps forward and clears his throat. He's a tall man with a familiar, if unfriendly, face. I look to the judge and find myself, for no reason whatsoever, admiring his posture. The prosecutor half-turns to the jury.

"You are charged," he says, his voice echoing with solemnity, "with the crime of being happy. How do you plead?" The 'do you' bit rhymes exactly. I've taken an oath to tell the truth. Everyone is looking at me.

"It happened without my knowing," I manage to say, because a part of me is suppressing the urge to cry.

"Are you suggesting, Sir, that had you known the day would make you happy, you would have done something to prevent it?"

"Yes," I reply. "I couldn't help it. It wasn't my fault. I normally manage to stop myself from feeling happy, but I couldn't help it."

A woman at the prosecutor's table suddenly stands up and shouts. I recognise her immediately.

"You have no right! After what you did, you have no right!"

"Silence in court!" the judge booms.

At school the next day, we are changing for PE when Garth, a boy whose teenage years have been ruined by a particularly bad outbreak of acne, and who normally faces the jokes that this creates without much bother, announces that he has lost his virginity.

"Wanking doesn't count," Thane adds.

There are general choruses of disbelief. "Come on, who is she then?"

"No-one you'd know. Just a girl I met at my parents' friend's party. Her name's Janine. She's my age. We did it in the garage."

We still don't believe him. Everyone laughs.

"Who'd want to have sex with you?"

"Laugh," he says. "I don't care. I know I did it. I don't have to prove it to you. While you are all still dreaming about it, I actually did it, so eff off."

For a brief moment, I entertain the image of him bouncing about on top of some poor girl, but it becomes too much to contemplate, and I look at the others, wondering whether to believe him. There's a look of suppressed envy on some; others shake their head in disbelief. I wonder how many of them have actually done it? A few have bragged before, but who is telling the truth? Unless the other half confirms it, we never can be sure. However, at our age, believing is easier than not believing. Having sex immediately elevates you to a rank higher than your peers. It makes you more grown up, as if it were some kind of secret club whose members all share the same secret. I too could make up a story, but I doubt I'd sound very convincing. We jog out onto the fields, still speculating about Garth's sex life.

I see Evelyn busy in her garden.

I hear a judge somewhere announcing a verdict of *Guilty*!

I wonder if she has found the shells. I want to call out and say hello, but I'm scared of what the others might say.

"Wouldn't mind planting my seed in her garden," one of my classmates says. The others laugh. The boy, his name is Andrew, continues. "I hear she's a fox under the covers. Hey, Calvin, didn't your brother say she was good in bed?"

Calvin's brother is Brendan, a senior with an infamous reputation when it comes to girls. It takes a while before I realise that they are talking about Evelyn. I find their tone distasteful. The more Andrew jibes, the angrier I become.

Don't ask me…

"Is that supposed to be funny?" I suddenly demand, confronting Andrew, who is a bit taller than I am. Before I know it, I've grabbed him by the shirt and push him to the ground. "She's a friend of mine." I punch him, square on the jaw. My first fight.

His response is quicker than I had imagined. Within seconds, the position is reversed – like I said, my first fight – and I'm soon unable to block the barrage of blows bashing into me.

Superman Thane comes to my rescue. He hurls Andrew off me and immediately asks how I am. Some of Andrew's friends hold him back. My lip is bleeding. My ear hurts. I'm not finished. I push Thane away and charge towards Andrew, whose knee stops me in the groin, and I fall over, tears streaming down my face.

"What the hell's going on?" Thane asks. "What's gotten into you?"

I look up to see if Evelyn is looking, but she's gone back to class. Thane helps me to my feet. I groan as I stand up.

"Are you mental? What on earth possessed you? He's far stronger than you are."

I try to explain, and then have to do it again before the Headteacher and Mrs Flank, who does not look pleased at all. I'm given a warning this time and told to behave myself. I wonder if this will affect my pocket money status? The fight was over so quickly that nobody remembers why it really started. They know it was because Andrew said something I didn't like, but nobody knows who we were talking about. They don't know her name, only some girl who slept with Calvin's brother.

The other boys look at me differently now. As if I'm mad. The crazy kid who attacked Andrew Howser during PE. My eyes are bruised; I look like Thane. He calls us "The Bruise Brothers". There's no reason for him to stand up for me, but he does. It's cool having a friend like him. I should tell him this, but I don't.

During Geography, I replay the fight again in my mind in slow motion. Except, in this version I don't lose. After school, just before going to see Mr Edwards, I stop off at Evelyn's garden to leave a few shiny pebbles I had picked up on the beach during my walk with Thane yesterday.

The shells are where I had left them.

"I heard about your scrap," Mr Edwards says. "I didn't put you down as a fighter."

"It was a moment of foolishness," I confess. "It happened without my thinking."

"It's your thinking that interests me." Mr Edwards leans forward. "Do have an hour to spare?"

I nod.

He says, "Good," and shows me the final year English Writing paper. "Choose a topic and write a poem about it," he says.

"Now?" I ask.

He says, "Yes, now."

The topics are pretty obscure, if a bit dull. The one that catches my eye is: "All pain is relative."

I think of Thane, of Auntie Wendy, of Thane's mother, of the fight. I close my eyes and breathe deeply.

The page is blank but not intimidating. I can do this.

Clear your mind; try to think of nothing.

Which is precisely what happens. Nothing.

Then… this is not my voice I hear.

This is the voice of some other me. An older me, who does not cry at nights or feel sorry for himself. And like the tears that I sometimes cannot stop, the words begin to flow.

Members Only by Christopher Elliot.

"I'll tell you what does hurt,"
says the man with the tattoo on his lips,
the man with the safety-pin through his eyelids, "this,"
and he shows me a scar where a nipple should have been,
points to a picture of a girl, of a weird earring.
"That's nothing," says the anorexic
whose husband left her for someone else,
someone thinner; whose fridge is full of rotting food,
whose certificates from the school of gourmet cooking
still cling to the walls, "let me show you the mother
of a girl whose unborn baby is dead inside her, then
we'll talk about misery." "Well done," says another.
"That gets me right there." And she coughs,
trying to get the fly out of the hole in her throat.
It's my turn.
I feel incompetent.

"All I have," I say, "is this,"
holding up a poem about a cat up a tree,
about a little boy's tears and the cold, hungry wind.
First, nothing.
Then,
"That'll do," they say,
leading me by the hand
to where it's warm.

I look up at the clock. It's taken me exactly 40 minutes. It's funny, while I was writing that, all I could really think about was my rock pool, and how much I wanted to go there. I hand it in and Mr Edwards asks me to wait while he reads it.

"You are condemned," he says afterwards, "to a life of torture."

The remark throws me.

"All thinkers are, and you are a thinker. You are also a talented young writer. Do you write much?"

"Not really," I admit. "I don't think my writing's very strong."

"Well snap out of it quickly. You'll be a fool to let your lack of confidence prevent your gift from developing."

"Does this mean I've won the poetry competition?"

"I cannot tell you yet. There are a few exceptional pieces that have come in. It's going to take a while."

My gift? I have a gift? How peculiar.

CHRIS ELLIOT: PEBBLE CHAMPION AND POET.

Deirdre's party is tomorrow night. I found an invitation in my locker. I'm definitely going. Marmaduke is not happy about the bruises, but I tell him the whole story and he smiles.

"She must be really nice," he says. I tell him that she's also very involved with James.

"Be patient," Marmaduke advises. "If it is meant to be, it'll be."

Thane thinks I'm going to the party to be with Deirdre. I've decided to go because I want to meet this James. I want to find out more about my rival. I want to discover his Achilles' heel – some flaw in his personality. Or maybe I just want to be around Evelyn outside of school, to see what she's like without a uniform. That sounds kinky, but I assure you it's not.

Christopher?

My fight has not affected my pocket money, and I go clothes shopping on Saturday morning. I spend ages trying on different outfits, looking like a new person each time I peer into the mirror. The bruise on my forehead is now just a scar, and together with the black eye make me look a lot tougher than I actually am. I can be whoever I want to be and oddly end up thinking about what others I envy are wearing. Street casual, smart casual, indifferent casual, beach casual, club casual, pseudo-intellectual casual, or, fashion casualty? There are so many *me*'s I can become. There are so many *me*'s that I am. It's like I am constantly trying on different faces to see which one fits. Posters declare you are what you wear. I choose some khaki trousers and a polo neck sweater. No, and a checked shirt. No, too country. The turquoise over-dyed shirt with the stone buttons. Smart casual. I want to look older than I am.

Why can't I be happy?

I try to clear my head. I will not let these thoughts control my mind. I will pretend I'm deaf.

I immediately put the clothes on when I get home and model various poses in front of the mirror, pretending the mirror is Evelyn watching me.

I mustn't fawn over her, because that will only lead to disaster. I must be nice. I try a few smiles to see which one I think she'd approve of. What if her boyfriend is everything I'm not? What if all of this is sheer foolishness because she's never going to break up with him and I might as well prepare myself by not hoping for anything and forgetting about her altogether? No, no, no. My mission is to get her to fall for me, and I have to be patient.

Christopher, I know what you are doing.

I shower long before I have to and spend some time looking at my nakedness in the mirror. I'm only 15. Evelyn is older, more experienced. Again, I think of the dog chasing a bus. What does he do with it when it stops? I think of the other boys in my class. Would Evelyn ever go for one of them? Would she choose someone with sexual experience? I don't believe she actually slept with Calvin's brother. Is she sleeping with James? Why am I thinking these thoughts? What is going on with me? Why does it take me half an hour to do my hair? Why do I use some of Marmaduke's aftershave when I don't even shave yet? I decide not to flex my muscles; I don't have any. If Mum were alive, she'd tell me I was good-looking. Now that she's gone, I can't tell.

Thane is wearing jeans and a dirty T-shirt. He tells me I look smart when he sees me just before we leave for the party. Marmaduke's asked me not to be home later than two. It is now nine. I do not pass judgement on what Thane is wearing. I envy his ability to be himself without worrying about what others think of him.

"Deirdre will be impressed," Thane says.

She lives in a large house with a swimming pool and comfortable garden. There is a self-contained cottage attached to the house and this is where most of the dancing takes place. There are coloured lights strung up along the walls. Lots of kids are swimming. I didn't think to bring a costume.

Deirdre is standing near the barbecue chatting to some older boys. Her face lights up when she sees me. She waves enthusiastically. I nod a hello in return. She motions us to come over, but meets us halfway. She scowls when she sees Thane, and then smiles.

"Welcome," she says, giving me a hug and a kiss on the cheek. There's a mixed crowd of juniors and seniors. A lot of them are smoking – not just cigarettes I gather – and nearly everyone is drinking. Thane heads for the beer and leaves us alone. I know he has done this deliberately. He is grinning at me now. He looks incredibly handsome.

"You look nice," she says, and I mumble a thank-you. She's not bad looking herself. "Even with a black eye. I heard about your fight. Still waters, hey? Do you want to dance?"

"Later," I say. "I'm going to get something to drink."

"It's a date then. By the way, I think the eye makes you look very rugged. It's very fetching." She smiles and winks at me. "See ya later."

I'm looking for Evelyn. Thane gives me a beer and we walk over to the dance floor. Everybody dances so well. No Evelyn, though.

"Anyone take your fancy?" I ask Thane.

I want to say "Yeah, you," as a joke, but don't.

"The night's still young," he replies. "But that's not the question. The question is, will I take anyone's fancy?"

We sit down.

"I don't see why not," I say. "You're good looking. I think you're good looking."

Careful...

"You don't count. But thanks anyway."

I want to ask him if he thinks I'm attractive, but I decide not to. Instead I say, and I'm not sure why, "How come you drink if you're against your old man drinking?"

"Because I don't drink every day, from the moment I wake up to the moment I collapse at night," he says, and I'm struck by the seriousness of his response.

"Sorry," I say instinctively.

"Don't worry," he says. "We're not here to worry about our parents. We're here to have a good time, remember? How come you decided to come to this party and not the last one?"

I shrug. "I was going through a rough time. I didn't feel like a party."

Because I did not want to be miserable company, and because at the last party I went to, I got drunk and ruined a friendship.

"You're a strange one," he says. "How can you possibly have it rough? You've got the nicest father in the world. Is it your mother? I know you don't like to talk about her. When am I going to meet her?"

I stand up.

"I'm going to dance," I say. "You?" I know he knows I'm avoiding the subject. "Like you said," I add. "We're not here to discuss parents."

After another beer, I relax a bit and don't worry so much about whether I'm a good dancer or not. Thane dances wildly and happily. The music is awesome. Well mixed, well balanced. Something for everyone. Someone taps me on the shoulder. I turn round. It is Andrew, my sparring partner from yesterday.

"How's the eye?" he asks. There is no sarcasm in his voice. He has no scars. "I hope I'm forgiven."

"I've already apologised," I say.

"Yes, but it's my turn now." He holds out his hand. "I'm sorry for the things I said."

It is then that it strikes me: he was just being a teenager shooting his mouth off. Nothing more. There was no malice in his intentions. I had overreacted. He didn't deserve a smack in the mouth yesterday. What got into me? Not that it matters; I'm the one who looks the worse for wear. Time and future relationships will alter his adolescent view of girls and sex. Weird thoughts again.

We join a small group of people from our class who pass around joints. I do not give it a second thought and pull on the joint when it is passed to me. This is my first time. The others laugh when I cough. The conversation is about sport. Our school's gone through to the finals of some tennis tournament. We speculate about our chances.

After a while, time wobbles, and I'm unsure how much time has passed. It seems like a long time. When I look at my watch, only a few minutes have passed. When I look at my watch a bit later, I find that half an hour has gone by. The talk eventually becomes silly, and I find myself laughing at stupid things. Thane is giggling. He does an impersonation of Mrs Flank and we roll about in stitches. People are splashing about in the pool. The music is just right: it's slowed down and become more reggae-ish.

"Don't drink any more for a while," Thane advises a bit later. I'm having a brilliant time.

Evelyn has arrived. Alone. No James. Unless he's already here of course, but I don't care, and call her name loudly, getting up to meet her. I stand up too quickly and have to steady myself. I'm not sure if she's hugging me or holding me up.

She's hugging me.

"Oh, your eye. Oh, you poor thing." She smiles warmly. "I heard what you did. That was so gallant of you. You're such a sweetie."

How did…?

She is looking radiant. Her eyes sparkle. Or mine do, I'm not sure.

"Where's your boyfriend?" I ask.

"He can't make it," she says. "He has to study for an exam on Tuesday. He's at college."

My heart sinks. He's much older than I. I stand no chance with her. Not even if I beat up everyone who ever mentions her name. She's very friendly towards me, though, which is nice. It's not me talking to her. It's some other me. The nice one. I decide not to ask her about the shells. I don't think she'll have found the pebbles yet. Deirdre spots us and comes running over. I don't mind. I'm in a good mood. She drags Evelyn off to meet some friends, which I do mind, and Evelyn gives me another hug, which I don't mind, and says that she'll catch up with me later. Deirdre reminds me that I promised her a dance first. Thane has been watching us carefully.

"Aah," he says. "The pieces are falling into place. Evelyn."

"Shut up, you," I say, grinning.

"You like Evelyn. Of course. It all makes sense. Why didn't you tell me?"

"Because she'll never go for me," I reply.

"Crap excuse. I'm your friend. You can tell me anything."

"She'll still never go for me," I say. Thane nods.

"Older women. Always a mistake. You're right, though."

More joints. Another beer. I feel a bit too heavy to dance, but when Evelyn and Deirdre call me over, I welcome the invitation. Evelyn dances beautifully, gracefully, with poise and elegance. Deirdre dances like she's on TV. Her eyes, I notice, look very large. If I dance too fast, I get giddy, so I slow down, like Evelyn. Couples around us are kissing. Evelyn looks ravishing. I now understand what the expression "So near and yet so far" means.

Curious thoughts swirl around my brain. Other voices tell me I'm not allowed to have a good time. I switch them off immediately and think of Mum and Marmaduke. I must not give up my resolve to make Evelyn like me more. I must show her only the best side of me. I must not pick on people who are stronger than I am. I feel like a swim and wished I had brought my costume. There's no way I'm swimming naked or in my underpants. I think of Darryl. Why, I don't know. I'm actually quite lucky, really. Look on the bright side. Vomit if said by Mrs Flank. Don't fall in love with Evelyn. If things fall apart, you'll only have to face the pain and the balloons all over again. Don't ever let anyone get close enough to make you fall apart if they should leave. No. Be positive. Things are not that bad. This is a cool party. I may not have a girlfriend, but I've got a new life with new possibilities. Forgive yourself, Chris. No, better not to think about it. Think about Evelyn, who dances like a… like a… c'mon, Chrissie, you're supposed to have a gift for writing… like a… sod it. In my condition, it's easier to think of clichés. Like a flower in the breeze. Vomit if said by Christopher? The music's fantastic. Deirdre dances close to me, presses herself against me. Evelyn just smiles. I wish Deirdre would go away. I wish I had the nerve to tell her how I feel. I don't care if Evelyn has a boyfriend. Maybe if she knew how I felt about her, she'd leave him for me? As bloody if. Maybe I should give up on Evelyn and go for more of a sure thing. Deirdre keeps smiling at me. I wonder if she's slept with anyone? Do I find her attractive enough to want to be intimate?

Do I?

"Hey, Chris," Thane says. "I need you to do me a favour."

He wants me to ask some girl if she likes him.

Deirdre has left Evelyn alone. I tell him I'll do it later.

"I'm curious," I say to Evelyn as we sit down at a table next to the dance floor. "How did you know about the fight?"

"Calvin told me. You actually punched someone because he was saying things about me? I'm very flattered."

"Well," I reply. "I didn't like the things he was saying about you because I think you're very sweet."

"You're so charming," she says. "You know Deirdre likes you?"

"I'm beginning to notice."

"She wants me to find out how you feel about her."

I shrug.

"She seems nice, I guess. I don't really want a relationship right now."

And then, when she asks me why, and before I have time to stop myself, I tell her the truth. I cannot stop the words. I tell her about Mum and the accident, about meeting Marmaduke. About how everything is still unreal for me. And I do it without wanting to cry.

Why I tell her, I don't know. I don't want her to feel sorry for me; I'm not looking for sympathy. Apart from Marmaduke and Mrs Flank, nobody knows about Mum. It's as if I need to tell her, need to tell someone.

Evelyn listens with concern. Instinctively, she reaches for my hand as I speak. I know it is not a romantic gesture. Her whole body tells me that she understands.

"I lost my real dad some time back," she says. "It's gonna take…"

"Time, I know."

"I used to hate it when people told me that, too. But it is so true, Christopher. It does get easier. And then it becomes a part of you, like a scar – a beautiful scar." Her voice is soft, and very very kind. "It hurts, and you will never forget this pain, ever. But you won't feel the pain, forever."

"Sometimes I do not want to get out of bed in the mornings. And I cry for no reason."

She nods.

"It's called grieving. That's why you cry. And you are supposed to cry. Don't worry about it."

I want to tell you what really happened. But I won't.

"How did you get through it?" I ask.

"Slowly," she replies. "I wouldn't be who I am if it wasn't for my father. He loved gardening and taught me all he knew. He loved his gardens and he loved life. And I realised I could keep him alive if I kept his love of life alive. Does that make sense?"

"Oh, yes," I say. I do not know if it is the drink or the joints, or just Evelyn herself, but just talking, without any hidden agendas, makes me feel better. The more she speaks, the more I realise just how lovely she really is. And I don't mean romantically. Yes, she is beautiful, but she has a gentleness, a kindness of spirit, a warm personality. Imagine how hard it must have been for her when her dad died. A huge part of me wishes to hold her, but not like that. She's so nice and been through so much, she deserves to be happy. It's as if I want to shield her from future pain. And if James makes her happy and treats her right, then she deserves that too.

Deirdre joins us when I get to the bit about Auntie Wendy's eloping. Evelyn looks at me warmly. She does not appear patronising.

Deirdre is straining to hear if we are talking about her, eager to find out from Evelyn what I feel. She's making me feel a bit uncomfortable. I get up, using the story that I need the toilet.

Thane finds me.

"Come on," he says, walking to the pool. "You have to ask her."

I don't mind. The girl in question goes to another school. Her name's Tamara. She doesn't fancy him. I break the news gently. He shrugs. I look at him closely, then across at Deidre and Evelyn. Then back at him.

What is going on?

"The night's still young," he says, going to get another beer.

Evelyn walks over and asks if I want to dance the slow dance, which has just started, with Deirdre. She smiles as she asks me. The beer and the joints reply that they don't mind. Deirdre holds onto me closely, and we dance clumsily until I realise that I'm supposed to take the lead. Over her shoulder, I see Thane and, just for a second, I wonder what it would be like to slow dance with him.

"I really like you," she whispers into my ear. The sore one. I must admit, I've dreamed about a scenario not unlike this one before. She presses herself up against me. "I wish you'd fight for me," she says.

I'm not being vain, but I think she's trying to kiss me. I pretend not to notice until the song fades. Then I peck her cheek. I really do need to pee. I excuse myself and make my way to the bathroom where, after unzipping, I look at my penis with a sense of anticipation.

I feel horny as hell.

Thane has stripped to his boxer shorts and is swimming in the pool. He calls for me to join him.

Perhaps I will.

I don't, however, because I see Evelyn on her own again, away from the dance floor. I wait until Deirdre looks away before joining Evelyn on the lawn, where she is examining some flowers.

"Hey, my little hero," she says. "Where's Deirdre?"

"She's still dancing. I'm doing my biology project on plants," I tell her, and go into detail about my research and findings. I know I should be stammering in front of her, being as I'm supposed to be in love, but it's not like that with me. The reason I like her is because she is so easy to talk to.

"Fortunately, my new dad is also mad about plants," she tells me. "He and my mum run a nursery near the station. Do you know it?" I shake my head. "I've always loved plants. They're hardier than you think, yet their beauty is so fragile."

I want to say something soppy, but I don't.

"Life is fragile," I say.

She smiles. "How are you really doing?" she asks.

I tell her, and once again, I'm not afraid to share my feelings. I don't, however, go so far as to admit having killed my mother, but…

Stop it.

In a split second, and without thinking, I lean forward and kiss her.

"You're so sweet," she says, smiling. "Christopher," and now she becomes serious, "don't put me on a pedestal. I really am flattered that you tried to defend my reputation, but I think it's only fair that you should know… the things Andrew said about me are true."

Thane is dive-bombing into the pool. He seems a million miles away.

"I did sleep with Calvin's brother. It was an act of sheer foolishness, and I regret it deeply. But I've forgiven myself and moved on. Don't build me up into an angel. I do have a past."

"You are what your experiences have made you, and I like you for it. But like I said, I'm not looking for love."

Liar, liar, liar.

"You're very sweet," she says. I don't mind her repeating it. For some reason, I know she means it. "And you're a handsome young thing. If I wasn't involved…"

This is said with affection, and I'm not hurt at all.

And that's the truth.

She looks up at a very good-looking guy of about 20 and says, "James, you made it."

Thane and I drink more as the night progresses. Evelyn and James join a group of her friends, but she smiles and waves every now and then.

I can feel my head spinning and decide to stop drinking. When Deirdre comes over, I ask if she has a pair of shorts so I can go for a swim. She says sure and leads me into the house to her brother's room. She explains that everyone is away for the weekend and won't be back 'til Monday night. She rummages about in a cupboard and finds me something resembling PE shorts.

Don't ask me.

Without thinking, I change into them in front of her. Perhaps that should be written in capital letters. As if it is the most natural thing in the world, I change in front of her, and make my way to the pool.

It is only when the icy water closes over me that I realise what I've just done. I let a girl see my dangly bits.

I sober up immediately.

Thane jumps in beside me.

"You'll never guess," I tell him. And I tell him.

I expect him to say something laddish, but instead he says, "Don't lead her on if you're not really interested."

"I'm not. I wasn't. I wasn't. I'm not."

"He doth protest too much," Thane replies, ducking my head underwater.

Deirdre goes back into the house and returns with a few towels. I pretend to be a dolphin and sink. Deirdre and Thane are speaking. Underwater, I open my eyes and look at his legs, his buttocks. I swim behind him and jump up to pull Deirdre into the water. She squeals as she falls in. Thane laughs loudly. Soon they both try to duck me, but the dolphin is too fast.

"I got changed in front of you," I tell her, although she already knows.

"I hoped it would happen sometime," she flirts, as we walk back to the house. And then she says, "You can go further than that if you want." Without a look back, she runs ahead into the house.

My heart races. I mouth the words, "Oh my God."

I've left my clothes in her brother's room. She goes to her room to change and is back just as I finish.

"Are you having a good time?" she asks.

"It's a cool party."

Split seconds and hours. This is a blur. Don't ask me what happens next. All I know is that we are suddenly kissing.

Just like that.

Suddenly, we are on the bed, and kissing and kissing. Images of Evelyn, of Thane, of dolphins flash in my head. All I'm thinking is: Oh, my God – I'm actually going to do it. How did we get this far? Who started it? Perhaps the swim was not as sobering as I had thought. She whispers that she has condoms. You're actually going to do it, my head says.

But my penis says otherwise.

Whatever sense of anticipation parts of me might have experienced earlier has been replaced by a sense of glum reluctance. I'm more embarrassed than I've ever been in my entire life. Deirdre is kissing me wildly and nothing is happening. She'll notice soon enough that parts of me are not that keen on this experience. What am I going to say to her? I've never had to deal with a situation like this before. Acute embarrassment is my first response. I try to think of Evelyn but I just feel guilty. I have to think of some excuse. Then I think of Thane, and his underwater buttocks. And something happens. What I tell her, before Thane opens the door, is, "I'm not sure if I like you this way."

The look of disappointment and mild confusion is heartrending. The look on Thane's face is equally disappointing.

"Sorry," he says, closing the door quickly.

Deirdre looks hurt.

I don't know what to say to her, except, "Sorry."

"I told you not to play with her feelings!" Thane says angrily. He is not amused. His eyes look wild. I'm too bewildered to register anything. "What did I just tell you? What the hell did I just tell you?"

"Shut up, you're not my mother," I retort, again – what is happening to me this evening? – without thinking.

"That's another thing." He turns around. "I've just found out about your mother. You lied to me."

He's drunk. He's going to turn into his father.

"Why did you lie to me, Chris? Why? I'm your best friend. I tell you everything."

"I couldn't."

"But I'm your friend." He looks like John did the day I shot him in the scrapyard. The day…

"Yes, well, there are a lot of things you don't know about me." I don't know why I'm being so defensive, or why I sound so curt.

"Apparently," Thane replies, almost, I think, in disgust, and he storms off.

I see Deirdre being comforted by Evelyn, but Evelyn does not smile.

It's time to go home.

Told you – never did like parties much.

Try to understand

I linger at the corner in the hope that Thane or Evelyn will come running, will ask me to return, but they don't. So much for keeping a low profile. My friend is angry with me, the girl I like thinks I'm a... I don't know what she thinks, but seeing the look on her face just before I left... Deirdre was so upset. Everything happened so quickly. Did I force myself upon her? Did I? No, it wasn't like that. She kissed me first, didn't she? Why then did I get undressed in front of her? Wasn't that leading her on? What will Evelyn think now? She knows I fancy her, she knows I'm not that keen on Deirdre. She must think I'm very confused. I shudder to think what Deirdre is feeling.

You fancy Evelyn? Oh, come off it, Christopher. Just be honest with yourself.

For a few minutes there, I was shoved into a world whose rules are secret and complex, whose boundaries are known only to a mature few. I floundered in inadequacy. Other boys would have risen to the occasion, would have taken control and would have stories to boast about on Monday. Have I drunk too much? Did the situation freak me out, especially after Thane caught us?

For a split second I entertain the idea that he is angry because he wanted to be the one I was kissing.

The mere fact that I was lying on top of a girl freaked me out, I think. Thane's arrival just made it worse. Would something have happened if Thane had not opened the door? Would I have overcome my feelings of bewilderment and later warmed to the experience?

I'm such a boy, still.

Maybe that is why Deirdre is so upset? Not because I told her I wasn't interested, but because I couldn't give her what she wanted? If that gets out to the others... I can almost hear the laughter in the changing rooms, the sniggers coming from the courtyard. Thane and Evelyn are not amused because I've hurt Deirdre's feelings. Marmaduke won't be amused either: it's two-thirty in the morning. I haven't angered him before; his reaction is unknown. I wonder if it will affect my pocket money? No, I think I have to do something monumentally bad before my pocket money is removed. Like what? Kill someone? Rape someone? I didn't rape her. She kissed me first. She led me to the bed. That's how it happened. How could I have raped her? I couldn't even get excited.

Deirdre is in the witness box, fighting back tears. The prosecutor asks her if she can identify her assailant. She points to me. The next witness is called. Thane steps forward. He explains exactly what he saw.

Why is he so upset? Oh, yes – he's also angry because I didn't tell him about Mum. But why should that upset him? Maybe it's because he has been let down by the people he cares about and my not telling him indicates a lack of trust?

Mother, you were right. I should have stayed at home.

And there I was, spending time in front of the mirror, hoping to make myself perfect for Evelyn. What a fool. Be nice? Let's see: Marmaduke will be angry I'm late. Thane is upset because I kept something from him and because I hurt Deirdre's feelings. Evelyn is upset because I upset her friend, and Deirdre probably thinks I'm a jerk. Not bad for my first party.

Marmaduke's asleep. He doesn't hear me come in. The trepidation I felt just before opening the door is unfounded. I catch a glimpse of myself in the mirror. It's not the same person I saw before going to the party. Where did everything go wrong? My new clothes fit uncomfortably now. I do not like what I see. I do not like what I see because I'm looking through the eyes of a hurt friend, a dead mother and a broken-hearted teenager. Where do you turn when everyone you know is angry with you? How do I purge myself of regret?

I strip naked and dive into the swimming pool. The water is cold. It is quiet and no-one is awake. Underwater, I swim from one side to the other. I am not sure how long I do this. It feels like hours. Soon I exhaust myself.

Pebble Champion my arse.

When I get out, I feel no cleaner than before. Every part of me yearns to speak to Auntie Wendy. She'll put things into perspective. But she's not here. Mum's not here. Nobody here understands how I feel. You would think that I feel upset. I don't. I feel angry. Angry that my world is so irreversibly different. That there is nothing I can do to bring Mum back, to return to the city and my old life. Angry that I could have been so stupid as to play around with the volume button in our little yellow car.

Angry because I can't get beyond this.

Maybe Marmaduke should share some of the blame? After all, maybe if he hadn't left us, Mum and I would not have been on that motorway that day? Look how successful his life is, while ours was a constant struggle to get by. How could he just leave like that? How could he just stop caring? But he talks about her with so much warmth. I suddenly remember the evening with Andrew, Graham and Sylvia. What if Marmaduke were... no, he's not gay... is he? Maybe that's why he and Mum...? I have to tell myself to stop being stupid. He can't be. He talks about her with too much affection. For some reason, I find myself racing to my room to find the postcard. I remember his reaction to the words.

I'm in love. Forgive me. Try to understand.

Understand what? Then another weird thought: what if I have got it all wrong? What if he left Mum because she was having an affair. The clarity of this thought unnerves me. Mum was cheating on him? The man on the farm. All this time I've blamed him for deserting us, when in fact, it was Mum who caused him to leave. I've had this image of a perfect woman, whose life was cut short because her son was being silly.

Maybe she wasn't perfect after all?

Do we have drink in the house? There are beers in the fridge. The thought of Mum cheating on Dad gnaws at me like a guilty conscience. There is so much I don't know. Mum wasn't unfaithful. She loved him. She told me so. I saw her crying. Perhaps she cried because of the guilt? The angle at which I view the world has been altered. She's not the person I thought she was. No, this cannot be. The woman I remember would never cheat on the man she loved. She was not that kind of person. The person I remember is… angry that I distracted her attention from the road and made her swerve into the lane containing the large shard of glass. I cannot let go of this.

Every morning, without fail, I'd wake up to the aroma of steaming porridge, toast, to her presence in the kitchen, to the warmth of her hugs as she'd see me off to school. I remember munching popcorn in the cinema on a Friday night, how we'd talk eagerly about the movie, how we'd re-enact scenes in the car on the way home. This woman would never cheat on her husband.

"Your move."

"I'm thinking."

"It's been five minutes, Mum."

"Well you play chess at school so you get much more practice than I do. Let me think. If I move my bishop here… Ah, but see what lurks behind that prawn – crafty little bugger."

She was always doing that. Deliberately misnaming the pieces. The rook became the crook, the bishop, the bee-shop, and the king, the thing.

"Mum, you know you're going to lose."

"Rubbish. I can't lose. I'm your mother. Sons are not allowed to beat their mothers at chess."

"Says who?"

"It's a universally accepted fact. Look it up. You'll see."

Another beer. I feel queasy. The toilet beckons.

I'm running towards the goalposts. Three defenders are in my way. Mum is shouting from the sidelines. "Go for it, Chris!" My mum is my biggest fan. She believes I can do anything. The look on her face is enough to make me try harder than my best. The ball soars into the back of the net, and I become a hero. Mum is beside herself.

Just before I get to his door, another thought stops me in my tracks. What if I don't really want to hear what he has to say? What if I am right and Mum really did have an affair? What if he really is gay? Oh, shit – do I really want to know? How will knowing this change things? We've been getting on so well so far. Do I tell him that I fondled some girl's breasts while actually thinking of Nathan?

Oh, shit – how much do I tell him? How much does he need to know? How much will others tell him?

Stop it, Christopher. Stop thinking so much.

Dad, I'm gay.

Before I know it, I've knocked on Marmaduke's door and let myself in. He turns on the bedside lamp and squints.

"What's wrong, Kris?" His hair is all ruffled. He sounds worried.

"I'm… I'm sorry to wake you."

"That's okay." He smiles. "Bad dream?" He sits up and invites me to sit down. "What's the time? You enjoy the party?"

It's almost four o'clock.

"I need to know why you left Mum," I say. He looks very concerned. "It's important for me to know. Was she having an affair? Are you gay?"

Marmaduke looks completely bewildered.

"Where would you get an idea like that?"

"I need to know. What you said about Auntie Wendy's postcard…"

He thinks for a while, then sighs, then smiles.

"It's not what you think."

"Tell me what to think, because I don't know. I don't know what to think." He can't smell the beer on my breath because I brushed my teeth after vomiting. I wonder if he knows I'm a bit drunk? A bit?

"Kris," he says. "Your mother and I loved each other very much. And I'm not gay. The words in the postcard – Sarah used those words, but it wasn't because she was in love with someone else. I'm not sure if you will fully understand this, but…"

"Then tell me. I want to know."

"Kris…" Again an invitation to sit. This time I do. "You know that painting is my life, and for a while, even before you were born, I found it harder and harder to spend time doing any art at all. I think, subconsciously, I had made a decision to devote my time to you and your mother completely. To the family. I didn't want to leave you. She made me. Your mother asked me to leave. Not because she didn't love me anymore, not because she was having an affair. But because I had stopped painting."

He sees me shaking my head.

"This is hard for me to understand," I tell him.

"Your destiny, I remember her saying, is to become a successful artist. And to do that you need to grow, and you can't grow in this environment. I have to let you go, to let you grow. She wanted me to leave because she honestly thought that I would not become a successful artist if I stayed. You've lost your passion for your art; I'm no longer your inspiration, she said. I didn't understand her at first. I thought she was mad. For a while I thought she was joking, but she had never been more serious."

Marmaduke's face keeps changing shape. I hardly recognise him at all. He sighs deeply. It's the second time I notice his wrinkles.

"One day," he says, looking away, "you had just turned five… no, wait… for a long time before that, I began to feel, well, trapped, if you must know. I loved your mother. I did… but I have been painting since I was ten… it's my whole life… and when Sarah had you, that whole life… I couldn't afford a baby and had to find a real job… that whole life disappeared. After a while I started to resent that. I began to feel… an anger that was completely foreign to me. I started shouting at her for no real reason… and you…" He looks up at me and then turns away.

Don't stop. Please don't stop.

"You… you were such a demanding child… there was never any quiet… work was annoying… Sarah was moaning…" He sighs again and then looks me straight in the eyes. "I beat her, Kris. We had another fight… our relationship was falling apart… I beat her. I smacked her and – I hope to God you don't remember this – I smacked you harder than I had intended…" His voice falters, and he tries to grab my hand when I move away. "That's why she wanted me to go. That's why I had to leave."

The silence that follows seems to shout at us. I can hear my heart beating hard. I have no idea what to think, what to feel.

"The man who I turned into was not the same man she married. The man who I am now is not the same man who left all those years ago. It has taken me a very long time to forgive myself for what I did, and there is a part of me that never will. But she forgave me. We did stay in contact, of course. You see, she realised I wasn't happy. That we were not happy together anymore, even though," he touches my arm, "even though we, deep down, loved each other."

"She forgave you? Why didn't she take you back?" My voice seems to echo in the room, while his seems to fill it.

"She forgave me for hurting her. I don't think she ever forgave me for hurting you. You mother was the wisest woman – the wisest person I ever knew. I was desperate for news of you, but she wanted a completely clean break, to help her cope. She wouldn't let me see you because she was afraid… that one time was not the only time I hurt you."

I don't feel drunk anymore.

"I know she loved me. You may not understand now, and someday I hope you will, but her letting me go was probably the hardest thing she ever had to do. I didn't agree at first, and it took me a while to understand, but if you see it as an act of pure unselfish love, then it might make sense. It was as if she saw us, ten years down the line, screaming and shouting. She didn't want us to end up hating each other. I didn't keep in touch because your mother wanted it that way."

"She told me you had gone overseas and were never coming back."

"I went to Paris for two years after we split up. Look, Kris… I guess this is a bit too much too soon. I was going to tell you everything when the time was right. And I want to promise you… and I mean promise you… I have changed so much since I left. I will never ever harm you, in any way, Kris. Ever. You have to believe me."

"Why did she send me to stay with you?" I ask, and there is a long pause before he answers.

He looks down.

"Kris," he says. "Maybe it's your mum's way of giving me a second chance."

Once back in my room, I realise there are now even more unanswered questions than before. Now that my head is on the pillow, it feels like I'm in a tumble-dryer. Thoughts swirl about, but can't escape.

I've no reason, and every reason, to cry.
I'm in love. Forgive me. Try to understand.

Another goodbye

The morning light seeps into the room and smacks me on the face. My head hurts; I don't feel well. I groan loudly. Hangover revenge. Typical. Ten-thirty. The world is alive and noisy outside, even for a Sunday. The balloon inside inflates and then changes its mind.

Enough tears. Enough self-pity. Enough of this.

The person who went to bed and the person who woke up are two different people. For a while I lie there absorbing the events of the night before, unable to put all the pieces together. No point calling Thane, or Deirdre. Marmaduke's busy in his studio.

So that's why he left us. I've gotten it all wrong. The world is not as I perceived it to be. I'm not who I thought I was.

My rock pool doesn't beckon – it positively yells for me to come over.

And just when I thought nothing could go my way… get this: someone is standing at the rock pool. I'll have to wait until he leaves.

PEBBLE CHAMPIONSHIP DELAYED

But he isn't leaving. He's about my height, I reckon. I wonder if I recognise him from school. I can't quite see his face. He bends down, picks up something, holds it to the light and throws it at the water. His pebble hops once, twice, three times, four times, five times, six, seven, eight times before it sinks. Taking my heart with it. I amble over the rocks, pretend not to notice.

HE DOES IT AGAIN.

This is war.

I find a pebble that feels just right and walk to the water's edge. He stops. He's seen me. I know he's watching. I recognise him from somewhere. He cannot hear the commentators in my head.

The best way to describe how I threw it is: poetry. The best way to describe how many hops it made is not to talk about it. I have to try again.

He picks up a pebble and waves at me. He throws the pebble and it hops four times before sinking.

That's better.

My stone hops five times and disappears. I look up. The boy's walked a bit closer.

"Chris?" he asks.

It's... whatshisname... Darryl from the bus. Darryl from...

"Hey, Chris!" He walks over and shakes my hand. "Darryl. Do you remember me? The coach from London?"

"I remember you," I reply, and before any of us can do anything, I give him a hug. Like a long-lost friend kind of thing. His hug is as generous as mine, and when he pulls back, he smiles from the heart.

"I was hoping I'd bump into you," he says. "Ah, you're smiling. Good. I don't have to try so hard this time." He is genuinely pleased to see me. I've done him no harm. He has no reason to dislike me. I can relax. I do.

"I keep thinking some poor fish near the surface is gonna get knocked senseless by these," he says, throwing the pebble in his hand at the water.

It bounces twice and then disappears. "What happened to your eye?"

"It's a long story."

You remember me... why?

"Every time I see you, you have some kind of bruise. There are organisations you could call, you know."

"My first and hopefully last ever fight. I'll tell you about it some other time. What are you doing down this way?" I ask.

"I felt like a walk on the beach," he says. There is something in the way he says that, that echoes in my mind.

"You want an ice-cream?"

There's a beachfront store nearby. A part of me is afraid he has something to do. A part of me doesn't want him to leave just yet.

"Oh, that would be magic," he replies, grinning. "I've been here since ten o'clock last night. I'm starving."

The pebble competition is abandoned as we walk to the main beach. It's almost eleven and the sun is already high. The beach is filling up with deckchairs and umbrellas and kids with plastic buckets. Teenagers play Frisbee, and I notice that I am more tanned than Darryl.

"On the beach?"

"Yeah. Silly really. I should have brought a sleeping bag or something. It was flipping cold."

"You slept on the beach?"

"Yeah, I was afraid I'd sink if I slept on the water. You deaf or something?"

I point to where I live.

"No point me knowing that now," he says. "Actually, I enjoyed it."

"On your own?" I ask, as we approach the store.

"Yes. Oh, it's a long, sad, sordid tale, let me tell you."

We enter the store and make our way to the ice-cream box in the corner near the window.

"What do you fancy?" I ask him, as we both peer in. I'm after a King Cone. We both reach in at the same time, and quite by accident, end up touching hands.

There is the slightest pause.

Anything can happen in a split second... before I pretend to grapple for an ice-cream and emerge with the cone. He chooses an ice-lolly, I pay, and we make our way outside.

Observers would not have noticed anything, but I am sure, in that second as our hands touched and he looked at me with a playful smile, that something happened.

Something.

Which is all in my head, because neither acknowledges anything, and as we walk towards the rocks, he tells me about his night on the beach.

"I thought it was going to rain this morning. Just before it got light, it clouded over and I thought: uh, uh – just my luck. But then it changed again."

"So how come you ended up there last night?" I ask.

"Like I said: long story."

"I've got all day, and I doubt it's a sordid as mine."

"Oh, mine's pretty hairy," he quips.

"Really?" I ask, in an all-knowing voice, and we both laugh.

"Yeah, that's pretty hairy too," he adds.

We sit eating our ice-creams on a rock near the water's edge. He is wearing a pair of khaki trousers and a big white T-shirt, with a green jumper round his waist.

"You surf?"

"Body surf, mainly. I don't have a board or anything."

"Must be amazing that, surfing."

"But you can't swim."

"How did you know that?"

"You told me, on the bus."

You wondered what it would be like to swim naked underwater. And now I wonder what you look like, naked.

"Oh, yes. No, I can't." He smiles. "You'll have to teach me."

"So how come," I say, using exactly the same intonation I did asking last time, "you ended up spending a night on the beach?"

"It's a long and sordid story," he says in a deadpan voice.

"Yes, we've established that… yours is long and sordid."

"So long it makes horses jealous."

"Gives them nightmares," I add, and he laughs.

"Very good – nightmares," he says. "Very corny. So, you like living here? What am I saying? Of course you do. You'd be pretty stupid not to. Better than the city. You said your dad got a new job, didn't you?"

"Amazing side-stepping of the question there, Darryl. But I'm sorry. I lied. My dad lives here. I was the one doing the moving. It's a long…"

"And sordid story," he interrupts. "Don't I know it."

"My mum died. I used to live with her in London."

Christopher…

"I am sorry to hear that," he replies. "Jeez, I'm really sorry to hear that." Then he leans forward and touches my arm. "Tough break.

How are you coping?"

I shrug.

"I have good days and bad days," I say. He looks at me – not with pity, but with understanding.

"I lost my brother three years ago," he adds, quietly. "I know what you are going through. It isn't easy."

"What happened?"

"Leukaemia. How did your mum go?"

"Car accident."

"Jeez, that's rough."

"Losing a brother is rough," I say.

"Yeah, but at least we saw it coming," he says. "At least we had a chance to say goodbye."

A seagull, attracted by the last piece of cone in my hand, hovers near expectantly. It can have it, but only if it takes it from me. I hold out my hand and wait. The bird is far faster than I anticipate, and the cone is gone before I know it.

"I broke up with my girlfriend yesterday afternoon," Darryl says. "Just before a mate of mine invited me to spend the weekend with him here. He lives up the road from you actually. But we had a stupid fight so I decided to walk off my anger on the beach last night, and I ended up staying. I was waiting to take the first train and ferry back, but the sunrise here is so beautiful I thought I would stay a while. I mean, how often do I get to come to the island?"

"You hungry?" I ask.

"Starving," he says.

"Oh, wow," he says, when he sees Marmaduke's artwork. "Oh, wow. You're so lucky. Look at this place. I wish my father was an artist. He's a plumber. Damn good one, too. Oh, wow – look at that." He goes over to a painting by the window. "It's almost alive," he says. "Look at the way the curvy lines intersect and seem to move away again. What is this? Some kind of blood system?"

"I think it's spaghetti."

"Spaghetti doesn't throb," he says. "This stuff wobbles when you look at it. Look at it. Don't you think it wobbles? Like some kind of illusion."

It's true. If you look at it from a certain angle, the lines on the painting – I still think it looks like spaghetti – do actually seem to move. I hadn't noticed that before.

"Oh, wow. Look at that," he enthuses. "It's like the closer you look, the less you see, almost as if your eyes lose focus, like you're looking at a mirage."

Marmaduke pokes his head around the corner. "I don't know who this is," he says, smiling, "but he has impeccable taste."

I move to introduce them, but Darryl cries out, "You're Marmaduke Elliot. You spoke at our school. Oh, wow. This is such an honour. You didn't tell me your father was famous."

I beam with pride at my dad. "He is?"

"You should see his work. Oh, but you do. You're so lucky. Pleasure to meet you, sir."

Marmaduke laughs.

"I'm not that famous. Nice to know I have a fan though, as young as you."

"You have two young fans," I add quickly. Darryl is overwhelmed. "I think a tour is in order. Dad?"

And so we show him the studio, and Marmaduke explains his latest commission. He now has six canvasses, all depicting different natural habitats. You should see the look on Darryl's face when, one by one, Marmaduke turns them around, and each time they blend with the composite picture, so that no matter how they stand, everything still fits together. It's hard to describe. Even I'm overawed at the cleverness of it. Marmaduke explains that once finished, the 12 canvasses (one for each month) will be exhibited on a giant panel, with moveable parts. "It'll be interactive," he says. "You'll be allowed to push buttons to rotate the canvasses of your choice. I'm quite excited by the project."

"He works all day on them," I tell Darryl, and he is clearly impressed.

Looking at Marmaduke through Darryl's eyes, I can see why he envies me. My dad is extremely talented. The more they speak, the more I realise how proud I am of him and how much of him there is to like and admire. How difficult it must have been to leave Mum and me. How many demons did he have to wrestle late in the night? There is still so much I don't understand.

"Will the finished collection have a title?" Darryl asks.

"It will, but Kris here has to decide." My father smiles at me and then offers to fix us an early lunch.

They get on famously.

So what if my friends are cross with me?

Something occurs to me as I listen to Marmaduke talk, as I watch the way he expresses himself, the way he smiles reassuringly at me. I cannot quite put my finger on it, but when the idea forms, and becomes clear to me, I'm struck by a sudden realisation. It's not a bolt from the blue; it creeps up on me like a whisper. A calm, irrational, undeniably beautiful thought. I no longer sense the balloons.

I have the best dad in the world. Darryl stays for lunch, and just after, Marmaduke produces a video he had bought in a charity shop. A documentary about the life of dolphins. I feel a strange sense of elation.

"Oh, wow," Darryl keeps saying, during the video. "This is incredible."

They are magnificent creatures. They have such beauty and look so innocent. Nature at its most guilt free, I think, and, for an hour, we are transported to another world.

I could wax lyrical about the dolphins, but if you close your eyes and see them yourself, you'll know how I felt watching them. I like being here with my new friend.

Afterwards, we walk along the beach. He removes his socks and trainers, rolls up his trousers and cools his feet in a rock pool.

"I have always liked dolphins," he remarks, "but I didn't like that part in the video where they showed you dolphins in captivity. All wild animals should be free."

"At least in captivity," I say, "they don't have to worry any more about sharks or fishermen's nets."

"But they are not free," he replies. "Wouldn't you rather have freedom over a fearless existence?"

"They seemed well looked after."

"Yes, yes, yes. But they're not free. How can they ever be happy if they are not where they are supposed to be? How can anyone? Imagine if your dad locked you in your room 24/7 and fed you like a king. Sure, you are well looked after, but…?"

"So you're saying we should not put them in aquariums?"

"Put yourself in their shoes," he begins.

"Dolphins wear shoes?" I tease.

He gives me a look: one that, at first, seems disapproving, but within a split second turns into a genuine smile.

"They should be where they were meant to be," he replies.

Where am I supposed to be?

'So how come you broke up with your girlfriend?" I ask, later. I've lent him a pair of shorts and we are on our way to swim in the shallows. It's a question I've been meaning to ask for a while. "Or did she break up with you?"

Stop fishing.

'I felt trapped," he says. "It's a typical story. She liked me, and that was enough, in the beginning, to like her back. But not enough to keep a relationship going. Are you involved?"

I laugh.

"Oh, no. I have other things to deal with," I say. He nods.

"I'm sorry," he says. "I forgot."

"How come you remembered me from the bus?" I ask. "I didn't say much."

"You remind me of someone," he says. But he doesn't go on to tell me who.

Darryl has a distinctly calming effect on me. It has been a brilliant day. The balloons have been replaced with bubbles of happiness. The joy of making a new friend. I screwed up with Thane and the others. I won't with this. As he speaks – his voice is so appealing – I can't help but wonder what lies in store for us. I'm sad, when at five-thirty he has to catch the train to go home.

But perhaps I'm telling it wrong. If you look at it another way, the day went like this: we didn't just speak without reserve, we played, pretending to be dolphins in the water. He was too scared to go too far out, but enjoyed riding the waves to the shore. We raced each other across the beach, played volleyball with a group of strangers – I think from a neighbouring school – chased each other across the sands and watched the clouds spin dizzily by. For one afternoon I completely forgot about my worries and fears. I'm happy I told him about Mum. He asked me about her, and do you know, I wasn't afraid to share some memories of her with him. Do you know what he said when I admitted that I found it hard to let go?

"You don't have to," he smiled. "She's a part of you now, like that scar. You'll always carry her with you, through the things she taught, through the memories you shared. If you stop living, so does she, to you."

I remember the words clearly and can still see the breeze ruffling his hair. He asked me about her, and do you know, I wasn't afraid to tell him. Memories of her and me, silly moments, came flooding back.

I'm ill. Mum is by my side. I think she is praying.

"Move over," she says, waking me one night, climbing into bed beside me. "Ruddy electric blanket's packed in."

"Way to go, Christopher!"

Christmas time and oodles of little pressies.

"Get over here, young man. How dare you leave this castle without kissing the queen goodbye? I demand a kiss, right now, right on the pecker." Smack. "That's better. Have a wonderful day, my darling."

I'm in the school concert. It is a serious business. She is in the wings, pulling faces, trying to get me to laugh.

We're dancing to Peter Skellern. We danced a lot, Mum and I.

The afternoon sun draws shadows along the ground. I don't want the day to end. Ever.

He tells me about his brother, the one who died, and there is so much love in his voice. He remembers their times together with fondness and a sparkle in his eyes. Why hasn't he let his brother's death consume him utterly, the way Mum's does me? Why doesn't he rage against the heavens?

"Your mum's accident was a terrible, terrible tragedy," he says. "But what is worse is if two people had died in that crash. I remember being angry when Thomas died: angry at God, angry at the world, angry at myself for not being a better brother. But then I thought: if he is up there looking down, then he must be so sad knowing he can't be with us anymore. And if he was looking down and saw me just give up on life when he had fought so hard to keep his – well, that would make him even sadder."

We have won our volleyball match. Our spirits are high. He checks his watch and tells me he has to leave soon. There is a sort of sadness, yes – but it is nothing compared to the joy I have felt all day. It is like neither of us wants the day to end.

"I want to tell you something," he tells me, as we make our way to the station. "The real reason why I came to the island."

"You needed space to think," I reply. "You probably felt bad about breaking up with your girl and needed some space to clear your mind. The beach is good for that."

He stops for a while and just looks at me. Like he is looking at someone else.

"What?" I ask.

"I had to decide something important last night. And I did, sitting staring at the moon and listening to the waves. And spending today with you has confirmed everything. I have had a really great time. Thanks, Chris, for such a nice day."

"Hey," I say. "I enjoy being in your company. I feel like I have found a new friend. Thank you for… breaking up with your girlfriend." We both smile. He knows what I mean. "So what did you decide last night?"

"To accept myself," he says, as we move on.

At the train station, while searching for his ticket, he remarks, "I want to give you something." He pulls out his ticket, but that is all. "You wanna know why I remember you and why I had hoped I'd bump into you again?"

I nod and shrug at the same time.

"Because you are beautiful," he says, leaning forward to kiss me on the lips. "Stay in touch," he says, and turns to board the train.

A lot can happen in a single moment.

I watch the train pull away. I wave as it disappears. Before, when we first said goodbye, I remember regretting that I had met him. Now, as I make my way back to the apartment and an empty room, my feelings are different. But I don't go back home. Instead, as I near my road, my walk turns into a jog, and the jog turns into a run. And I am running along the path towards the beach, and I am running along the sand towards the water. And I am swimming towards the swells, to where the waves are breaking.

And Mum, if you are looking – that's me, over there, the one with the huge smile on his face, the skinny one diving into the waves, the one who is so happy he could burst.

It was more than just fun; more than just the way we spoke, the things we said. It was the way he made me feel, like I was someone special. I envy the way he tries to look at life differently, at a slightly different angle. No, I don't envy him. In fact, he envies me and my life by the sea. It's strange, being a bit sad and happy at the same time. Happy that I've made a new friend; sad that he has to go.

Perhaps that is how I should view Mum's death. Happy, because my life would have been poorer for not knowing her; sad that we can't be together now.

For a while I'm not sure what to do with myself. I sit and stare at my bedroom walls. I try to decide what colours to paint them.

It's time I did something with this room.

Perhaps I should do some more work on my biology project? I've already dissected and sliced bits of the plant to examine under the microscope. I know how it works: photosynthesis, pollination, absorption of nutrients through the roots, the root system. I understand the processes and technicalities of the plant. But I don't know the plant.

I wonder if Darryl were to choose this topic, how he would approach it. I smile when I recollect his joy at seeing Dad's paintings. smile, thinking of the kiss. I make my way to the studio and gingerly knock on the door. Dad is making dinner. I offer to help, but he says he wants to make me something special.

For a long while I stay in the studio, rotating the canvasses quietly lost in my own world.

PEBBLE CHAMPION RETIRES

Chris Elliot, former world pebble champion, announced this afternoon, after a failed bid to retain the title — spectacularly stolen by newcomer Darryl Martyn — that he intends to retire from the sport. The only reason given, he claims, is to devote time to his biology project, which is due in less than three days.

Two days have passed. Deidre and Evelyn are ignoring me at school. Apparently, Thane is absent. I'll see him when I see him. Right now I must get my assignment done. For some reason, I want to do well so Darryl will be proud of me.

It is just after eleven at night. I've finished page six of my assignment. The telephone rings. Marmaduke knocks on my door.

"It's Thane's dad," he says. "He wants to know if you know where he might be. Kris, he still hasn't come home from the party."

The ground opens up and swallows me whole.

I tell myself to stay calm, but I can't. Panic rises within me. For some reason I cannot help but envisage the worst-case scenario. Something terrible has happened to my friend. He drank too much that night. Anything could have happened. There were drugs at that party; maybe he got involved with something he shouldn't have? I feel guilty, as if I'm to blame for his disappearance.

Am I?

No, I tell myself this is not the time for self-pity. My friend's lost. I have to do something. Thane's father is disappointed I can't help. He tells me he's called Deirdre's place and he's not there. Nobody saw him leave. I hear Thane's mother in the background, telling him to call the police.

Maybe he met some girl and went off with her? Maybe he's run away. Maybe he is hiding. Maybe he went home, slept, and left before his parents woke up? Maybe he's at Alex's playing pool? I have to phone Jedd to get Alex's number, and I don't know Jedd's number. Who else is he friends with? I don't even know where Alex stays.

An hour later, I call Thane's house. His father answers immediately. He thinks it's Thane. I tell Marmaduke that I want to search the beach. I think I know where he might be.

The winds have picked up and sand spits against my face. I don't know why, but something tells me to go towards the little beach we had been to on the bank holiday – the one that is only accessible at low tide. What if he went there, slipped on the rocks, hit his head and… No, I must not think like that. I call his name as loudly as I can, but it is drowned by the wind. What could have happened? Where is he? I slip on some seaweed and graze my leg. The wind is uncomfortable and it is getting cold. There is enough moonlight to see by, but not enough to see things clearly. When I get to some open sand, I find myself running and growing hoarse from calling his name.

If something awful has happened, how am I going to cope?

I will not blame myself for this.

The waves send spray over me as they crash against the rocks. Moving too quickly, I fall and hurt myself again. I want to stop, to go home and to pretend this isn't happening, but some stubborn thing inside me propels me onwards. There are no thoughts of superheroes or improbable commentators raging in my head. All I can think about is how I'm going to respond if the worst should come to the worst. I should have told him that I think he's a great friend to have; I should have listened to his advice about Deirdre. I should have been a better friend.

If Thane were sitting on some planet somewhere, watching me, would he laugh when I rage at the moon and call his name?

I call his name until I'm exhausted.

I am in my room, hugging my knees. I have left the door open so I can better hear the phone ring. I told myself that I wouldn't cry, that he is safe somewhere, that I am being silly. The balloon inside presses hard, and I can feel the tears at the back of my throat. But I am not going to give in.

Perhaps everything will be all right in the morning.

It is not. The day drags on second by hour-long second. Nobody knows where he is, nor where he could be. There are police cars outside the school.

I haven't slept yet. Desperately I've been wishing for the phone to ring.

Odd that he should talk about death so soon before disappearing. I could not escape thinking about the vibrancy of my self-appointed best friend, thinking about his infectious humour. Darryl was right. It's the impression we leave that is important. I hope something bad has not happened. I'd hate to lose a friend like him. I wish he were here so I could tell him that. That his friendship is important to me. I fear the worst when I see the Head talking to the police officers.

They ask to speak to me, and I tell them that I last saw him heading for the dance floor after shouting at me. I tell them we were fighting about some girl. For the rest of the morning, I'm numb and very, very tired. The school is buzzing with news of Thane's disappearance. Everyone is asking me where he is, as if I should know.

I question Alex, but he says he hasn't seen Thane all weekend. Deirdre is quietly getting on with things, pretending I don't exist. I want to talk to her, but she asks me politely to leave her alone. Of course she doesn't know where he is.

At break time, I see that she and Evelyn have joined the others in the courtyard. Given my embarrassment at the party, I don't think I'll risk encountering them today.

Our RE teacher leaves us with this message: "It's not what we become or achieve in life that is important. It's who, why, and how we love that matters. It's all that matters." All that matters to me, however, is finding Thane. That's number one. Number two? Bed. I'm so tired.

If Thane were here, I would tell him he was proof that he was wrong. We are not passing the time. Everything is food for everything else, he said, or did I say that? Anyway, I'd tell him that mankind does have a purpose other than to propagate the species, or to become compost. We all affect each other in our own ways.

Mum may be dead, but the impression she's left lives on. Thane has every reason not to be kind to the world, but he befriended me, the new boy, and made me feel less alone. What have I done for him? If he was here, I would tell him that his life matters to me. If he was here, I would show him.

At the end of the school day, I make my way to the Head's office and enquire about news of Thane.

There is none.

On the way to the school gates, I pass Evelyn's garden and find her patiently talking to her plants. I'm apprehensive about how she'll react to me, but she looks up and smiles. Her beauty is so radiant. I tell her there is still no news, and ask about Deirdre.

"Don't worry about Deirdre," Evelyn says. "She'll get over it."

"I honestly did not mean to hurt her," I confess.

Evelyn frowns.

"What do you mean?"

"What do you mean?" I ask.

"Didi's very embarrassed, that's all. It'll take her a while to get over it."

"Why should she be embarrassed?" I thought of my limp performance.

"You know, coming on to you like that. She knows you don't like her in that way. She was just a bit drunk, that's all. She thinks you think the worst of her."

I'm speechless. And all this while I've been feeling so guilty about Saturday night, convinced that she hates me.

The topic quickly moves back to Thane. I apologise for interrogating her and she politely reiterates that she has no idea where he could be. I tell her how worried I am, and she nods sympathetically. She even gives me a hug, although I wasn't fishing for one.

"I've gotta go," I say, preparing to walk away.

"Oh, and Chris?" She stands and, reaching for my hand, presses something into my palm.

It's an acorn. Just an acorn. I look at her, confused. What am I supposed to do, start a forest?

"No matter," she says, "how much that little acorn wants to be an apple tree, no matter how hard it hopes and how fervently it prays to one day bear apples, it will always be an acorn. And if nurtured and treated right, it will grow into one of God's most wondrous creations. I just wanted you to know that, Chris," she says, smiling.

The world does not behave in the way I expect it to.

"And give Deidre some time," Evelyn says, pulling at the weeds. "She just needs some time."

Standing at Thane's front door, with the sky ever greyer and the wind as strong as last night, I feel a tremendous weariness come over me. All the wasted energy worrying about what others might be thinking. I can be such a fool sometimes. There is no reply and I knock again. Poor Thane, what a life he must lead. How lonely he must be. Listen to me, I'm talking about him as if he were alive.

Listen to me, I'm talking about him as if he were dead.

I knock again, and again there is no reply. If he is alive, I'll tell him that he need not feel so alone. That I'm his best friend. Until some higher purpose comes along, I'm sticking with my policy of trying to be nice.

If I thought the balloon had disappeared, I was wrong.

I knock on the door again, almost banging, but to no avail. I don't care if I have to face Thane's father again. The worry is beginning to eat away at me. There are tears in my eyes as I make my way to the gate. The side door leading to the back garden is open. That's where they are. His mother's probably hanging up washing, trying to lose herself in housework. The old man's probably in the shed – yes, the door is ajar.

No mother in the garden, though.

I remember Thane telling me that his father liked to retreat to the shed to get away from the shouting. It all falls together. They must have had another fight – probably blamed each other for Thane's disappearance, and why not? It's their fault, not mine, and she's not opening the front door because she thinks I'm her husband. If the worst has happened, imagine the guilt they'll feel. Do I really feel like an encounter with the old man? Despite my better judgement, I peer through the crack in the door.

I see Thane, standing on a chair, with a rope and noose in his hand.

Pretend everything is in slow motion. I push open the door, thinking: this is not right, things are not so bad that you have to do this. I will not let you do this. I dive at Thane, calling his name, pushing him backward against the wall. We fall in a heap.

"You cannot do this!" I'm shouting at him. He looks bewildered, amazed, terrified. I don't know why but I'm punching his chest.

"You can't do this. You can't do this. You can't kill yourself. Things are not that bad. I'm your friend, for God's sake! You can't leave me. You can't. You're not allowed to. I don't care what you have done, I forgive you. I forgive you. I forgive you. Whatever it is, it's not your fault, Thane. You must forgive yourself. It's not your fault! Jesus, I'm so happy you're alive."

I'm hugging him hard; I don't think I've ever been so pleased to see anyone. "I'm so glad you're okay!"

Real time: Thane pushes me away.

"What the flip are you blabbering on about? Forgive me for what? It is I who needs to forgive you for stealing the girl I care most about." Thane stands up. "Forgive me for what? And who said anything about killing myself?"

"The noose..."

He looks up and laughs loudly.

"Yeah, well there's another one on the other side of the shed, you fart. I'm fixing a hammock for my old man."

He's right. There is the hammock on the floor. The noose is for a knot to hold the steel ring in place. I'd laugh if I wasn't so embarrassed. I'd be embarrassed if I wasn't laughing so much.

"Where have you been?" I ask after composing myself. "Do you know the whole world is looking for you?"

Thane grins.

"Apparently, my folks do give a shit," he remarks.

That night I have the best night's sleep in ages. Dreamless sleep.

When Thane wakes me the next morning to walk me to school, he says, "I thought I'd enjoy some time with the simple things in life – like you, for instance."

He has such a cute smile.

Me, cactus

I think Marmaduke will enjoy my biology presentation. Evelyn too. Thane's project about sharks is graphic, gruesome and utterly compelling. I have to follow that with my investigation of a plant.
Typical.

Everyone is pleased to have him back. Even Deirdre hugged him. Apparently, he spent the time away with a friend on the mainland. When he returned from the party, he heard an almighty row coming from inside his house, so he decided: screw it, I need to get away from here for a while. He wanted time away from the world. He wasn't angry with me on Saturday night; he was jealous. He's liked Deirdre for ages. Deirdre's not angry with me; she's a bit embarrassed. Evelyn's not angry with me.

I'm not angry with me.

All that worry and concern.

I spend so much of my life worrying about phantom fears, about things that never happen. I need to chill a bit. Learn to like the weedish parts of life. Embrace its unpredictability. Talking of which, Mum's ashes arrived yesterday. Marmaduke and I are going up to the white cliffs. He says there is a spot she used to enjoy as a girl. We're going to say goodbye to her there.

And I found out Marmaduke had been sending us money for years. Mum kept it all in a savings account for when I need to go to university.

Auntie Wendy sent me another letter yesterday. She's definitely getting married. She confessed that she had met her fiancé three weeks before Mum died and was meaning to tell me, but after the accident, didn't think it appropriate. Apparently – I've checked with Marmaduke and he confirms it – I was unconscious for nearly four days after we crashed. The last few weeks… How long have I been here now? A month? Seven weeks? The last few weeks have been weird. So much has happened. Time has shot past quickly in slow motion.

Just before it is my turn to present my project, I think of Darryl, and I smile. I look up at Thane and he holds up both thumbs.

Salt of the earth kind of person, him.

Here goes:

Oh, I was meaning to tell you about the thoughts that occurred to me while Darryl visited on Sunday. You know how last time I had to speak to the class, I was so nervous? I'm not nervous now. I'm not a criminal, condemned to a life of guilt. I'm not a weakling, unable to control his emotions. I'm a teenager with lots to discover. I looked at Marmaduke that morning, listening to him talk with such passion about his work. I looked at him, and when he looked at me, I knew that I was home, that someone cared for me. That I wasn't alone. I knew not only that he loved me but also that I really loved him. And then, on the beach, after the dolphin video, it struck me, while Darryl spoke, that the reason Mum wanted me to stay with Dad is so simple: she still loves him and wants her love for him to continue through my love for him.

I'm part of an incredible love story.

Mum would not want me to spend the rest of my life feeling miserable. She does not look down on me in anger. That's not her. That's not the mum I know.

When she let Dad go, she did not fall apart. She knew she was doing the right thing. She did not descend into self-pity and blame herself mercilessly. She loved life and lived it passionately. She loved me with equal intensity.

I know I don't remember her face sometimes, but I will never forget her incredible capacity to love, to forgive.

The car skids. She's not holding onto the wheel. She's holding onto me. Her final moments are spent trying to protect her son.

For a while I thought that I would be incapable of loving someone, that my heart had become as hard as a pebble. I thought that if I loved someone and they left, my life would be empty. Now I see it's the opposite. I didn't kill Mum. She's not angry with me. I can feel her now, rooting for me, encouraging me from the sidelines. Keep going. Keep life alive. Appreciate your friends. Hold on to what really matters. Time is too short. Don't worry about what it's all about. Live meaningfully. Because, I've realised, the purpose of life is not to reach goals, or become something. It's about being true to yourself, about making some kind of meaningful contribution to the world around you. When a pebble hops across the surface of the water, it makes an impression, even if it touches for the briefest of seconds.

Life is too short for insecurities. Juliet may have killed herself when Romeo died; when Dad left, Mum poured all her love for him into me. She wants me to grow to love him. That way her love for him will not die. It's a part of him, a part of her, a part of me.

I've thought of a title for Marmaduke's exhibition. He's quite pleased. I've chosen the title:

Us.

He says it fits perfectly.

Time to do my oral presentation. Here goes:

I don't talk about the inside of the plant. I don't show slides of the root system. I pretend, instead, to be a ladybug, fussing over the need for shelter. I put on a voice and pretend to be speaking to my little children. Then I'm a bee, smudged with pollen, dripping with honey. Now I'm an ant, using the stalks as a highway to the petals. And now I'm a spider, spinning my web beneath its leaves. Now I'm the soil, holding onto the roots as the downpour washes mud away. Mr Bird impatiently tells the plant to grow so he can build a nest within its branches. Miss Cow likes the plant because it contains nutrients not found in grass. Mr Caterpillar rushes along; he's been spotted by Mr Bird. Each voice I use is different. I try to include as much humour as possible. Walt Disney could not have done it better.

I am a cat, chasing a squirrel up a tree.

I am a squirrel, showing the cat an almost rude sign.

I am the hornet, protecting my nest.

I am a monkey, looking for a place to sleep.

I am a tiger whose claws scrape the bark. I am the sap that oozes to make it all better.

I am the leaves that cover the autumn soil.

"Understanding anything in nature," I conclude, "does not mean taking something apart to see how it works. I've been doing that with myself for too long. To find out what makes a plant so important, take it away to see what gap it leaves behind. To know what it's about, listen to the voices of its neighbours. I can tell you loads about the cell structures and waterways, tons about the mechanisms of its existence, but unless I tell you how it relates to everything around it, you will not understand why God put it on this earth. The weed is part of an incredible love story. I started investigating a plant. I ended up discovering something about life."

The presentation is an enormous success.

Marmaduke's paintings have helped me to understand how everything fits together. I think of Evelyn and her acorn. I think of Thane and his crush on Deidre. I think of me and my crush on Darryl. I should have taken his telephone number.

Imagine a plant committing suicide because the weather is too severe, because raindrops hurt. Does it feel bad when Mr Bird eats the caterpillar off the leaf? Does it blame itself for being part of life? Does it stop growing because its neighbours have been uprooted?

At lunch break, I make my way to the courtyard. It will be my birthday soon. Break is saturated with birdsong and pupil chatter. Deirdre is sitting with a few seniors under the shade of an oak tree; Evelyn is staring up at me. She says something and the others look up.

"Hey," one of the girls shouts. This time Deirdre says something and the girl goes quiet.

I'm holding something behind my back. I almost want the girls to start their comments, the usual crap. I've thought of a brilliant retort involving cellulite, but I don't hear any insults.

My heart is beating rapidly, but there is no noise in my head. This is something I have to do.

"I have something for you," I say, holding out a potted cactus, blooming, which I bought from Evelyn's parents' nursery. The flower is a vivid purple. "To say no hard feelings."

There is a look of panic on Deirdre's face, as if I'm going to tell all about last Saturday.

As if.

"It's a cactus," one of the girls sneers.

"It's beautiful," Deirdre says. She doesn't know it yet, but Thane's planning on asking her out, finally.

"Just don't hold it too close." I hope she understands. "Friends?"

I also tell Evelyn not to worry about the weeds in her garden. If she makes a place for them, the insects will be less likely to harm other plants. It's just a theory, but I feel like telling her that. I'm a teenager, what can I say?

"Give them a place, make them feel at home. They too have something to contribute. Thank you for helping me realise that." It sounds corny, and I'm convinced a snide remark is imminent. It is only when I walk away that I hear Evelyn shout, "Thank you for the shells. They're lovely, and the pebbles."

Live each day as if it is your last? Nah. Live each day as if it is your first.

When I get home, I find a letter from Darryl on my bed. He must have posted it the next day for it to have arrived so quickly. In it, he says some really nice things – like thanks for the afternoon and how he really wants to see me again. He wants me to teach him how to swim and has left his phone number and asked for mine (result!). When I write back, I am going tell him how much his kiss meant to me – and accept his request to teach him to swim.

I decide to tell Thane about my feelings for Darryl.

As I fold the letter to return it to the envelope, something else drops out. It's a newspaper cutting.

Watch me smile.

DRAMATIC BIRTH ON BUS

There's my picture. I'm behind the ambulance men. I had almost forgotten about this.

I read further. Darryl has highlighted the bit where they say that the woman had named her baby boy… Chris… after the name on the towels a kind stranger had given her.

Typical.

Oh, by the way, I came second in the poetry competition. I won't tell you who won. But it'll be me next year.

You'll see.

If you enjoyed this novel, feel free to leave a positive comment via the author's website:

www.alandavidpritchard.com

Printed in Great Britain
by Amazon

37053655R00108